# CONFEDERATE
# TREASURE
# COVERUP

# Other Books
# by
# Peter Viemeister

---

**The Beale Treasure**
*NEW History of a Mystery*

**From Slaves to Satellites**
*250 Years on a Virginia Farm*

**Historical Diary of Bedford, Virginia, U.S.A.**
*From Ancient Times to U.S. Bicentennial*

**A History of Aviation**
*They Were There*

**The Lightning Book**

**The Peaks of Otter**
*Life and Times*

**Start All Over**
*An American Experience*

# CONFEDERATE TREASURE COVERUP

## DUTY, HONOR & DECEIT

A NOVEL
BY
PETER VIEMEISTER

2004

HAMILTON'S

BEDFORD, VIRGINIA 24523

*Confederate Treasure Coverup: Duty, Honor & Deceit*

Published by
Hamilton's
P.O. Box 932
Bedford, VA 24523
www.peterv.com

FIRST EDITION

First Printing: August 2004

ISBN 1-883912-18-0

Library of Congress Control Number 2004108769

Printed in the United States of America

# CONTENTS

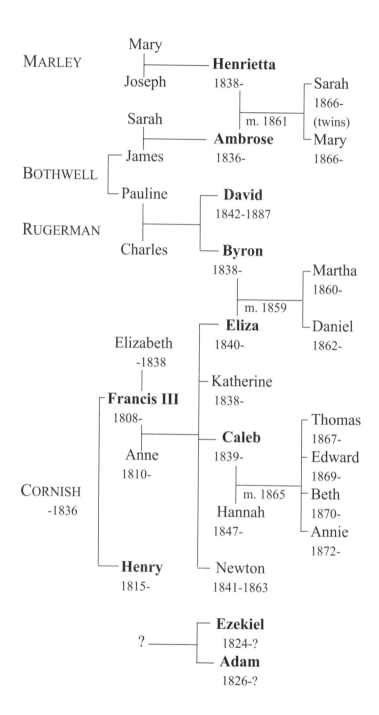

MARLEY

Mary

Joseph

**Henrietta**
1838-

Sarah

m. 1861

**Ambrose**
1836-

Sarah
1866-
(twins)

Mary
1866-

BOTHWELL

James

Pauline

**David**
1842-1887

RUGERMAN

Charles

**Byron**
1838-

m. 1859

**Eliza**
1840-

Martha
1860-

Daniel
1862-

Elizabeth
-1838

Katherine
1838-

**Francis III**
1808-

**Caleb**
1839-

Thomas
1867-

Anne
1810-

m. 1865

Hannah
1847-

Edward
1869-

Beth
1870-

Annie
1872-

CORNISH
-1836

**Henry**
1815-

Newton
1841-1863

? 

**Ezekiel**
1824-?

**Adam**
1826-?

# TO WHOM IT MAY CONCERN

This story, told to me by certain relatives involved in a complex enterprise, the nature and details of which they vowed not to allow to be known for 75 years after the death of the last survivor of the group in order to protect innocent family members, has been held in trust for more than three decades. My mother, the last survivor, passed on in May 1929. The Trustee, ███████████████, and/or its successors, is therefore authorized to release this manuscript in the year 2004.

Martha Rugerman
Lynchburg, Virginia
October 1929

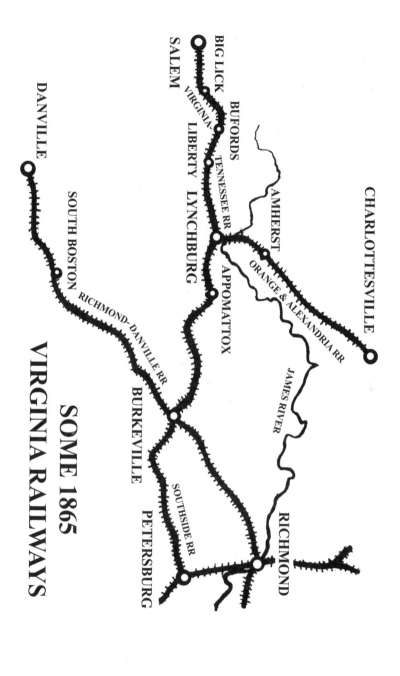

SOME 1865
VIRGINIA RAILWAYS

DANVILLE

BIG LICK

SALEM

BUFORDS

VIRGINIA

LIBERTY

TENNESSEE RR

LYNCHBURG

SOUTH BOSTON

APPOMATTOX

AMHERST

CHARLOTTESVILLE

RICHMOND-DANVILLE RR

ORANGE & ALEXANDRIA RR

JAMES RIVER

BURKEVILLE

PETERSBURG

SOUTHSIDE RR

RICHMOND

# CHAPTER 1

# *Richmond*

The 1865 March morning sun struggles to penetrate the haze of mist and smoke blanketing the besieged City of Richmond.

Colonel Ambrose Bothwell, Chief Auditor, and his cousin, Captain Byron Rugerman, Director of Treasury Operations, stride briskly up the hill to the Capitol for a hastily scheduled 8:30 Wednesday meeting with their boss, George Trenholm, Secretary of the Treasury. They sense something urgent; normally he met them at 9:30 on Thursdays.

This building, elegant symbol of dignity and tradition, designed by Thomas Jefferson and resembling a classic Greek temple, is about to lose its role as the seat of power of a weakening Confederate States of America.

Up the steps, between imposing columns, the bearded young officers salute the guards and enter the big portals, then stride into the dim and dank main hall, ignoring the dust and grit that has accumulated on the marble floor during the siege. They march side by side, heads up, chins down, with the poise developed as disciplined cadets at Virginia Military Institute in Lexington, Virginia.

Bothwell, 29, the taller of the two, was class of 1857 and had enlisted early in the war, in 1861; Rugerman, two years younger and a year later. Bothwell's wife, Henrietta, is back home in Lynchburg. Rugerman's wife, Eliza, lives with her parents and her two children on her family's modest farm in

Bedford County. Their gray uniforms are tidy, not really clean, but at least dust-free from a good shaking.

At the conference room door, eagle-eyed staff assistant Lt. Coleman waves them in. "Secretary Trenholm is expecting you." Rugerman smiles at the aide as he steps by. Bothwell nods.

From inside, a rich baritone voice calmly and quietly says "Come in, please."

Trenholm, a tall man with wavy silver hair, had been staring out the window. He gestures for the officers to sit at the table and quickly steps to the door, "No more visitors, Lieutenant."

"Good morning, sir," says Byron Rugerman.

"Good morning, sir," echoes Ambrose Bothwell.

The room is chilly. The furnishings and even the men look haggard in the gray morning light, filtered and diffused by unwashed windows. There is a feeling of foreboding.

Trenholm slides a chair close to his visitors. He leans both big hands on the table and flexes his fists. As he sits down, the Treasury Secretary looks at the door, lowers his voice and says, "I have a special challenge for you."

The Secretary exudes confidence and leaves no room for debate. His fine dark suit has wrinkles, as if he had slept in it. But his authoritative manner befits a successful banker and shipping magnate, whose ships have been eluding the Union blockade. This man knows that money is power, and he understands how to raise or borrow it, and how to use it to get what is needed. President Jefferson Davis respects his judgment. Trenholm, in turn, has found he can trust and rely on auditor Bothwell and operations director Rugerman.

Straight faced, Bothwell responds, "Yes sir. What is it, sir?"

The Secretary begins, "I have just come from Twelfth Street and a special Cabinet meeting with President Davis in the Mississippi Room of the White House. You know our Confederacy is having a difficult time. Very difficult. We had hoped—indeed we prayed—that we could keep the Federals out of Richmond. The President is very reluctant to leave." He paused a moment and then continued, "We've lost many men. Too many. The people are hungry. The train that takes wounded to Lynchburg is the only one that returns with food and supplies. The O&A Railroad from Charlottesville to Lynchburg has been cut off. Much of the V&T track from far western Virginia to Lynchburg has been cut off. Southside rails to Petersburg are being cut off. We get some supplies from Danville, but not enough. Citizens are leaving any way they can. Our soldiers are hungry and exhausted."

Trenholm looks troubled as he takes a breath and solemnly adds, "It is inevitable that we will soon have to leave this noble city."

"Do we know when?" asks Col. Bothwell.

"Federals are approaching from the northeast and the southeast. General Lee advises that Petersburg will not be able to hold them off much longer. We are terribly outnumbered. "

He pauses and briefly scans each of the officer's eyes.

"President Davis and I agree that we should be ready to move our government further south, to Danville. We don't know exactly when, but move we shall, probably within the week. As you know, Mrs. Davis has already gone. Mrs. Trenholm and my daughter, Mary Josephine, chose to stay with me. Some officers are in Danville right now, planning on how to accommodate us when we get there."

"Yes, sir. What is it that you want for us to do? Shall we go on ahead to Danville?" asks Bothwell.

Trenholm leans closer to the officers and, barely audibly, says, "I want you men to take care of some of our treasury assets...but not at Danville. Let me read part of some recent messages that General Lee sent to the President. In one he advised *Everything of value should be removed from Richmond.* In another he made this suggestion: *I think Lynchburg or some point west the most advantageous place to which to remove stores from Richmond.* What do you think?"

Bothwell nods and answers, quietly, "Lynchburg was a key Federal objective, but it escaped ruin when General Hunter backed away last year."

Rugerman calmly adds, "Lynchburg is indeed a haven. And tracks between here and there are still in place. Both the Colonel and I are from Lynchburg."

Trenholm interrupts, "Yes I know you are. I read that in your department records file. And I know that both of you know how to get a job done. I also know that you are Free Masons and can be trusted. That's why I am talking with you now."

"We want to do everything we can."

"President Davis and I have decided to take General Lee's advice. We want to store some of our treasury assets in a safe place, a secret place where it won't be stolen or seized by the Yankees. This will be our treasury reserve. Then, when the tide turns, we can use that reserve to help our recovery." He looks again at the closed door.

Bothwell focuses in, "What do you mean 'some treasury assets'? What kind and how much?"

"Our government needs the bulk of our assets to pay our people and pay our suppliers in the months ahead. So most of the treasury assets go along with me to Danville." He pauses and looks at Bothwell, "Davis and I studied your audit update of last week—and I'm not talking about our paper money—we think we should store about $100,000 in reserve for the future."

"That's about one quarter of all the hard money we have. For compact handling, I suggested, and the President agreed,

4

it should be primarily gold coins. And we do have them, don't we?"

Bothwell calculates, "That could be 5,000 double eagles or better yet, 10,000 eagles. Yes, we have more than enough eagles."

"All right. Your mission will be to take that reserve west and store it in a safe place. We have valuable jewelry, too. Take some of those pieces, too. It could be useful in negotiations. And keep enough coins handy to pay for what you need."

"This has to be kept secret. The President knows and I know. Now you two know. I don't want anyone else to know. The Federals will be looking for our assets. Your moves must be secret. Where you put it must be secret. We don't want it stolen, and we don't want the Yankees to get it. It isn't my money or your money. It belongs to the people of the South. You must protect it at all costs."

Bothwell does another small computation in his head and concludes that the gold coins could weigh about 400 or 500 pounds. He begins wondering how to secretly transport—and hide—that much weight. He thinks to himself that even removing it from the Treasury vault will involve risks. The Yankees aren't the only ones who would like to get their hands on it—some citizens might as well.

The Secretary continues, "I need a workable plan. The future Confederacy is at stake. We have to be ready to go within the week." He looks Bothwell in the eye and orders, "Bring me your plan Friday morning, by noon. Can you do it?"

Bothwell glances at Rugerman, pauses for a moment and carefully replies, "Yes, sir, we can do it. However, sir, we may need one or two others to help us."

"All right." He leans back. "You do what you must. But secret. Very secret."

Rugerman adds, "We will be careful, sir. We can do it."

Trenholm stands and extends his right hand to Ambrose. As they shake, Ambrose thinks to himself, "I have big hands. I had forgotten that the Secretary has the biggest hand I ever shook."

Then Trenholm grips Byron's hand. Trenholm thinks, "Here's a man who knows how to shake hands—he's confident—I like that."

Trenholm leans forward—and proposes a tighter schedule, "9:00 A.M.? Earlier if you can."

# CHAPTER 2

## *Team*

Once outside the building, Bothwell looks at Rugerman and says, "We will do it, Captain—Byron." It sounds more like a question. Rugerman takes a breath and replies, "Yes, sir, Colonel—Ambrose—sir. If it can be done, Colonel, we can do it. We sure can try." They look at each other and very slowly nod, then slowly nod again, and then briskly nod once more.

They start down the steps and head for their office.

Byron, reassuring himself, looks at his older cousin and says, "Remember when your father asked us boys to relocate a big woodpile in a single day? It seemed hard, but we said we could do it. It was hard, and we succeeded. I thought we had finished it. Then Uncle James said, 'That's not good enough. Square up the pile evenly.' We had to work another hour."

Ambrose slowly shakes his head. "Yes, we finally did get his approval, at least partly. I still don't know if he thought we did it completely right. That job was easier than this. We didn't have to keep it secret. What Trenholm wants us to do is a complex mission, sort of like the imaginary tactical missions we were assigned by 'Old Jack' when he was teaching at VMI. Only this one is real."

Byron's eyebrows move up, "And really important. There's a big risk here, too. The Yankees—and others—would be willing to kill for it. We can't let anyone know we have it. If Jackson were here now, he'd make it very clear that we must complete this mission—without fail."

Ambrose stops, and confides, "Secretary Trenholm never lacks confidence. He assumes that the Confederacy will revive. I just don't know. Let's be realistic. It may be all for nothing."

Byron responds with, "It may be possible."

"Revival or not. We have a job to do. I'm sure we can do it."

Byron muses, "Maybe this war will end soon. I really miss my family. Martha is such a good child. I don't even know my little Daniel. He was born after I left home. You know, at night it really weighs on me. I miss Eliza—her hugs, her enthusiasm, her warmth, her love."

"Yes," replies Ambrose, "I miss Henrietta, too. My wife is a fine woman. We plan to have a family some day."

"I'm ready for this assignment. It's better than staying in Richmond. We will be doing something for the future of the Confederacy. Hopefully it won't get bloody. So far, we have been spared that kind of pain."

Ambrose starts walking again, "Captain—Byron—this mission is something we are meant to do. Let's get started on our plan in order. Get your ideas ready."

Thomas Jackson—"Old Jack"—and other VMI faculty had etched their minds with a sense of honor and duty. They had also learned about strategy, tactics and coordination. They know that two of them could not do this mission by themselves. They brainstorm a strategy which involves as few people as possible, probably close relatives who were loyal to the South and completely trustworthy.

Byron says, "With the right help we could move those assets to Bedford County near these Blue Ridge Mountains. We can disguise what we do and not attract attention. We can make something work."

Ambrose says, "Every step, every move, must work perfectly."

Already on the Treasury staff are two men they know and do trust: Byron's younger brother David and Byron's brother-in-law Caleb. Ambrose and Byron believe that, together, the four of them will be able to do it.

The four men convene in Bothwell's stark conference room in the Treasury Building, shut the door, and sit on straight back wooden chairs around a small conference table. They will develop a detailed plan.


The senior man, the official team leader, Colonel Ambrose Bothwell, seems taller than his actual six-foot height, in trim uniform, erect, with closely trimmed dark beard. Proud of his family roots in Scotland, he is the only child of James Bothwell, Lynchburg attorney and politician, and an adoring mother. He speaks with almost too much certainty, accustomed to being special, and enjoys directing others. A voracious reader, he devours works by Poe. Twice since he was a boy, he had read *The Gold Bug*, fascinated by its intricate intrigue. Math and accounting came easy. At the Marshall Freemason's Lodge and from his father, he learned respect for the due process of law and the ethics of fiduciary responsibility.

At VMI in Lexington, he graduated with 23 others on July 4, 1857, then joined his father's firm as a junior partner for finance. Four years later, at age 26, in early spring, he married a childhood friend and fellow Presbyterian, Henrietta, daughter of minister Joseph Marley, who claimed some sort of kinship going back to John Calvin. They live on Diamond Hill, not far from his parents, in a compact home which his father had acquired during an estate settlement. Henrietta is a volunteer nurse at one of the hospitals. She has help keeping her house. Joshua Singleberry, owner of eleven slaves, rents out Rebecca, a middle-aged woman, to come each Friday to clean and do the wash, as she had been doing for the senior Bothwells for years.

This tranquil situation was shattered in the spring of 1861 when war broke out between the States and Ambrose volunteered for the Confederate army. Henrietta accepted his decision calmly, showing no emotions. Like her husband, she would be a good poker player—if she were to play cards at all. His fellow enlistees elected him Captain, and his skills led to being called to serve in the Treasury office.

Bothwell is an analyst, orderly and thorough, more pragmatic than philosophical. His cousin Byron Rugerman is creative and action oriented. Byron will be second in command on this mission.


Capt. Byron Rugerman, 27, Episcopalian, eldest son of gregarious Charles Rugerman, a prosperous Lynchburg tobacco and food broker and wholesaler, and Pauline Bothwell Rugerman. The Rugermans buy locally and from the West, and sell locally and to the East. Byron has sandy, curly hair; he is sturdy, muscular with athletic grace. A friendly, confident smile and quiet baritone voice command respect in spite of his undistinguished five-foot-eight frame.

Byron enjoys challenges. His mind nimbly explores possibilities and sets goals and finds one route or another to reach them. He rarely seems to doubt himself. A natural leader, he readily accepts responsibility, and, like his Freemason Lodge brethren, father and uncle James, he keeps his word. His younger brother, David, obeys him as he would his own father.

The Rugerman family owns no slaves and believes that slavery is, at best, a peculiar institution. They question the justice of it, but make no effort to alter the economic system which depends so heavily upon slave labor. James Rugerman encouraged his sons to appreciate and be respectful of all people who work for and with the business. Byron and brother David were comfortable chatting with the slaves who handled the tobacco bundles and rolled the hogsheads at the Lynchburg market and who unloaded produce coming in on the Virginia and Tennessee Railroad from the West and on the Orange and Alexandria from the North.

In boyhood, Byron and David had been fascinated by trains. They would spend hours around the rail yard. They watched the cars as they were uncoupled and recoupled to form new trains. As teenagers, they would greet the crews of incoming V&T and O&A trains with fresh coffee for the engineers and conductors. Over the years they got to know many of them by name.

In a VMI class of thirty graduates, Byron Rugerman proudly received his diploma on July 4, 1859. Institute Superintendent Smith handed him his certificate and, as he did with other graduates, presented him with a small Bible, advising, "Let this be your guide."

A week later he married Elizabeth ("Eliza") Cornish, a Bedford County farm girl whom he had met two years earlier at a wedding of mutual friends in Saint John's Episcopal Church in Liberty. Byron's VMI classmate, Charles Steptoe, an aspiring clergyman, was among the well wishers.

The young newlyweds resided in a wing of the senior Rugerman's home on Fifth Street. Eliza missed the scenic vistas of her family's farm, though the smell of manure on the streets provided a link to her rural heritage. It was the year when Lynchburg renamed its streets. Byron had to keep reminding himself that, though he had not moved, he had a new address: Clay Street. He began working for his father full-time. He always liked helping out at the family business and had been entrusted with adult tasks when he was still in his teens. Food retailers found him to be a good man who treated them fairly. He could charm a hostile or unhappy customer into a mutually agreeable solution.

Byron became a father when Eliza gave birth in April 1860 to daughter Martha. This was the first grandchild of Pauline and Charles Rugerman; little Martha did not lack for attention or anything else.

In early 1862, Byron and younger brother, David, joined the cause. Byron was elected Lieutenant, David a Private. Eliza moved to Buford's in Bedford County to help her parents and do a man's work at the Cornish farm. In August of that year, Eliza delivered a son, Daniel. Within a year, as Byron's managerial skills and charisma became apparent to all, cousin Ambrose called Byron to join the Treasury staff in Richmond and elevated him to Captain. He also called Byron's brother David, to serve as an aide. Byron called Caleb Cornish.

Caleb Cornish, now 26, older brother of Eliza and still a bachelor, is average height, with dark hair and a weathered complexion, physically strong, lover of living things, quick to act but slow to speak. On the Cornish family farm he learned right from wrong and his place in his community and his family. Ever since he could walk, he followed his father Francis around and grew to love nature and animals, from animal husbandry to stealthily stalking game for the table. Unlike many other Bedford farmers, who own a half dozen or more slaves, Francis Cornish owned just one slave, middle-aged Ezekiel. Caleb was grateful to have someone working alongside him with all the needed physical labor. He enjoyed working up a sweat and having the satisfaction of getting things done.

Caleb believes that the war from the North threatens his homeland and family farm. His sense of duty and desire to defend Virginia, his family, and especially to protect his younger sister, led him to enlist. Though starting as a private, his outdoor know-how, quick step and keen eyes helped him and his squad survive a year of scouting missions into Yankee territory; he moved up to Sergeant and then 2nd Lieutenant.

Brother-in-law Byron knew Caleb's unquestionable integrity and had him called to join the Treasury office in 1863.

Caleb and the Cornish family still grieve the terrible consequences of war. In 1863 Caleb's younger brother Newton died in action, and the family does not know where. Caleb's sister, Eliza, hopes beyond hope that he is still alive, somewhere. Caleb represses his sadness and anger and vows to do everything he can to avenge Newton and to end the conflict. He so yearns to be back at the farm.

Ambrose, Byron, and Caleb know well David Rugerman, the fourth, the youngest, and most cooperative member of the Treasury team. David is a likable young town boy of average height, beardless, sandy-colored hair and complexion which has been spared the ravages of outdoor life. A bit soft of body, gentle of voice, he was steeped in traditions of southern loyalty. Teachers and classmates at the Lynchburg co-op school honed his reasoning, but it was his parents and older brother who provided his philosophical foundation and taught him to listen and to watch. He grew obedient, looking to his father and big brother for guidance and leadership. He believes in trade with the North and even Europe. He shares the compassions of his mother and sympathizes with the slaves he encounters. Nevertheless, he believes that abolition, the ending of slave labor, could ruin southern prosperity, and he firmly supports Virginia's independence and the Confederacy.

Admiration for his older brother moved David to enlist with Byron in the Confederate army in 1862. His too-large eyes quickly learned how to squint when he was taught to aim his rifle. He learns quickly, and seems eager to please his superiors.

In spite of his youth, David, now 23, nevertheless has a keen understanding of human nature, enriched during his frequent visits to the rail yards and markets, seeing commerce in action, bosses motivating, and merchants negotiating. He envies his big brother's ability to persuade people to do what he wants. David will be a helpful member of the Treasury team.

# CHAPTER 3

# *Ready*

In the small conference room in the Treasury building, the four men discuss their mission behind closed doors.

Ambrose reviews the basic ideas, "When we leave Richmond, all the Treasury assets will be together. The train, with Davis on board, will be heavily guarded. Once underway, we have to divide up the treasury. Most of those assets will go to Danville. The 'reserve,' Secretary Trenholm's goal, 10,000 eagles, is to be stashed west of Lynchburg. I figure that is about 400 or 500 pounds of gold coins. All the rest goes on to Danville. "

"We four are the ones to do this. Each of us will have an important part to play. Byron. Caleb. David. Good to have you. I shall be in charge of course. I'm the auditor. I'll go with the main Treasury to Danville; David, you will be with me. Byron and Caleb, you take the coins to Bedford. You must move and hide the reserve assets without drawing attention. We can't let anyone know what we are doing. We must confuse people, trick them to think we are doing something else."

Byron muses, "Fooling people? Deceit. We will deceive. Isn't that strange?"

"Strange?"

"Yes. Strange. Our parents taught us to be always truthful. And at the Lodge we vowed to avoid hypocrisy and deceit. But now, we will. On purpose."

Somewhat defensively, Ambrose replies, "Yes, we will deceive. But this is different. It is necessary. We'll still be true to our brethren. Our mission is for the good of Virginia, the good of the Confederacy. To get it done, we must divert attention, even if we lie to some people we encounter."

"Strange," says Caleb. "It will take some getting used to."

"We have to do it."

Shaking his head, David asks, "Does it bother you at all?"

"Of course. But our cause is just. So we do it."

"I guess so."

Ambrose continues, "Our trail must not lead back to us or the reserve. And we must be consistent in our stories."

Byron says, "If we have to get help, we may have to pay them. And we sure have to distract them from what we are really doing. You know, like a magician. Make them look the wrong way."

Ambrose gets back to specifics, "One problem is how Byron and Caleb can handle 400 or 500 pounds of gold. Certainly not in saddlebags!"

Caleb adds "And not by wagon, either. That would take forever."

Ambrose states the obvious, "We have to use trains. But which trains? How?"

Byron answers, "I've checked the latest rail reports. We know the rails from Richmond to Lynchburg are open. Hunter did tear up the track at Liberty last year, but it's been fixed. Tracks going west to Big Lick and Salem may or may not be open. West of there is not good. However, we can get into Bedford County. The telegraph is working through Lynchburg and Salem."

Byron and David share their knowledge of trains and railroad operation with the others.

Byron points out, "There is no direct train from here to Bedford. Even if there was, it would leave too easy a trail for anyone who is following us. We'll have to change trains and change cars to get where we want to go. And we will have to change the stories we tell people as we go along."

"That's true, Byron. You and David work out how you could get there in stages. Now, what do we do about splitting up the assets and transferring the bags of coins? How can we do that so that people don't notice?"

Byron volunteers, "I've been thinking about that. The train will be moving. No one but us should be in the car. No saddlebags. We'll use boxes. You know, wooden crates—manageable size." He pauses and then continues, "My idea is this. Not just ordinary boxes. Coffins. No one looks inside coffins."

Ambrose is surprised. "Coffins?"

"Yes, coffins."

David reacts, "That's a great idea!"

Just then Caleb stands up. "Wait. Stop. I think I heard someone at the door!"

Ambrose orders, "Go, see."

They hear sounds of someone running away in the hall.

Caleb opens the door, looks both ways, and reports, "I'm sure someone was there. But he's gone now."

Ever the optimist, Byron guesses, "He didn't hear anything. No one else will know our plans."

Ambrose looks at Byron, "Captain, let's hope you're right."

Then, speaking more confidentially, he continues, "When you go through Lynchburg on to Bedford, then what? I see no reason to involve our families in Lynchburg. But Byron, your Eliza—yes—she is where we need her—in Bedford County. We may have to alert her that something will be happening. Byron, you know how she thinks. You will have to get a message to her that will let her read between the lines without anyone suspecting a thing."

Byron proposes they send a wire to Eliza:

> To Francis Cornish at Bufords.
> Train bringing remains of Newton & cousin Albert.
> Have wagon ready. Caleb

Caleb says, "My sister is smart. She knows we have no cousin Albert. This will alert her that something is up."

David frowns, "Why does Caleb sign it? Byron, you're her husband. Why don't you sign it?"

Arms open, Caleb cuts in, "Think about it, David. Blood is thicker than water. It's logical that I bring my brother home. It would raise fewer questions that way. I think Byron is right. Anyway, we'll send that telegram at the right time. But not yet."

Nodding, the others agree, "Not yet."

The team then works out a detailed scenario of steps and timing.

Bothwell cautions, "Everything is going to have to go just right. None of us can slip up on what we have to do. We all know there is high risk of being discovered or failing altogether. Good is not good enough. It has to be perfect. Remember, the enemy can be anywhere. And even here in Richmond there are desperate people who could try to interfere. We may have to make changes as we go along. But, God willing, if we do our job carefully, the mission will succeed.

David responds, "Yes, sir. You can count on me. I'll do whatever you need me to do."

Caleb, ever itchy for action, says, "I hope we do it soon...I want to get going."

They wind up before midnight. Byron suggests, "Sleep on it. If you see any holes, or ways we can improve our chances, let me know. We'll meet again tomorrow at 5:00 A.M. and run through the details again."

Bothwell says, "Then Byron and I will brief the Secretary on Friday at 9:00 A.M. as he requested."

Ambrose Bothwell and Byron Rugerman are waiting outside Trenholm's office at 8:30. When he arrives just before nine, he ushers them in immediately, looks up and down the hall, and shuts the door, "You have a plan?"

"Yes, sir," says Colonel Bothwell, "We do. It involves Captain Rugerman and me, and just two others here in Richmond: Captain Rugerman's brother David and his brother-in-law Caleb Cornish, both of whom you know. This will be done with utmost secrecy.

"On the day you leave for Danville, all treasury assets will be on the train with you. David Rugerman and I will accompany you to Danville with the bulk of the assets. Now this is important: along the way, some assets—the 10,000 eagles-worth you suggested—the reserve—will be dropped off and taken to safe hiding by Captain Rugerman and Lt. Cornish."

"Good. Don't forget to take some of the jewelry, too. It could be converted to cash some day. And each of you should have a goodly supply of ready money, for whatever you might need. Fill your pockets. "

"Yes, yes, we will do that."

"Where will you hide the reserve? Lynchburg?"

"No, sir. West of Lynchburg, in Bedford County, sir. We have it worked out."

"Who will know exactly where?"

"Besides us, only our key operatives in Bedford—Eliza (Captain Rugerman's wife) and her father. He has a farm. They can be trusted."

Bothwell, proud of the plan they had conceived, continues, "Now here's how we'll get it done." He begins to unreel the details of how it will work.

Trenholm stops him, raising both palms.

"I trust you," he said, "Don't tell me how you're going to do it. Just do it. I'll tell the President that you've a hiding place and a way to get the reserve there. We've many other decisions to make. The President will be the one to decide when it is time to move out. Probably in a few days. And when I know, you'll know."

Trenholm stands up and moves to open the door. "Thank you."

"Thank you, sir." They answer as if a single voice.


During the next 48 hours, the team of four choreographs and rehearses details again and again. So much will depend on the railroads, yet the system is deteriorating daily.

News from the battlefields worsens. The haze over the city darkens as smoke drifts from faraway Petersburg. Occasional artillery fire sends a faint rumble, like distant thunder. Everyone knows that Richmond will fall. No one knows exactly how soon. But soon, surely.

The veneer of civilization peels away with the impending chaos. Citizens are fleeing the city any way they can, mostly on foot. Some are pulling carts filled with personal belongings. Starving pets are left behind to join other cats and dogs dying on the streets. A boat, if one can be found at all, would be useless: the river is controlled by the Federals. The only horses to be hired are sick or starving. As police leave, shopkeepers abandon their wares to looters who help themselves with impunity. The Army soldiers guard only government offices. Most civilian government personnel and families have already headed south.

By Sunday morning, April 2, 1865, it is evident that Federal forces are mounting a massive attack on Petersburg and moving on Five Forks. Petersburg has been the barricade protecting Richmond from the hordes of Federals approaching from the southeast. A message from General Lee, delivered to Davis at the morning service at St. Paul's Episcopal Church, advises that he can no longer protect Richmond.

Davis bows his head and remains absolutely still. He seems far away. He is taking stock of the state of affairs of his precious Confederacy and weighing options for the future. Surrender?

No! He decides to move his government immediately to Danville and continue the fight.

Then he sits bolt upright, with head high. He rises and walks out, accompanied by two armed personal aides.

By midday, a haggard but calm Davis announces that it is now time to move. All government groups begin implementing their evacuation plans.

President Jefferson Davis's order triggers a flurry of frantic activity. Colonel Bothwell is just one of many who sets a team in motion.

# CHAPTER 4

## *Connect*

An eerie mix of fog and drizzle envelopes the soldiers surrounding the rail station yard. Lanterns bob along, with people heard but not seen. There are a half dozen trains being assembled, but two special trains stand ready. One is the usual ambulance train, destined for Lynchburg. The other looks anything but presidential, yet is tightly guarded, ready to take Davis and the Confederate government to Danville.

Most window glass is missing in the second passenger car. The train is dirty, except for the foremost passenger car in which will ride the President and his key cabinet and staff. With more lamps than other cars, its interior glows as testimony to the attentiveness of the presidential staff. At the end of the train are two aged baggage cars. The forward one is the Treasury car. It will contain the assets of the Confederate treasury. Caleb Cornish is already inside. The last baggage car, older than the other, was inherited from the severed Petersburg to Carolina line.

The sound of murmuring voices and clattering shoes mixes with the sizzlings of the engines.

Passing through the guard line, David Rugerman returns from the treasury office where he has assured Colonel Bothwell that the Treasury car is ready and that the end baggage car is "all set."

Byron stands near the two baggage cars, directing officials on by towards the passenger cars ahead. David notes, "I think

I recognize that Lynchburg ambulance train conductor from several years ago."

Frightened citizens press against the guards, begging to be given escape from the city. All the pleas seem the same, "Help me. Help my children. My baby. Please help us." The soldiers know their duty and grit their teeth. The pleas are ignored.

Soldiers check Cabinet members and their families carrying bags filled with their most precious personal items. They scurry along and then squeeze into the passenger cars up front. Byron recognizes the Postmaster and Secretary Malloy.

Suddenly, piercing the general din, is the sound of gunfire from about a block away. First two shots and then six or seven more.


Groups of agitated citizens, held away from the Treasury building by soldiers, had been intently watching as boxes and bags were loaded onto three wagons and covered with tarps. Tipped off, or merely guessing, the onlookers believed that precious treasury gold was about to leave the city. The three horse-drawn wagons were indeed laden with bags and boxes of coins, ingots, script, and even jewelry which had been donated by Southern women to help the Confederate cause. Soldiers marched alongside and Bothwell, commander of the treasury transfer mission, rode aboard the lead wagon. Clusters of citizens followed, intimidated and held back at a safe distance by the soldiers.

Once the convoy was rolling, the guards seemed to be looking more ahead than behind. Then, four men, followed a few paces back by a pack of hopeful looters, rushed towards the end of the convoy and attacked the guards at the last wagon. Two swung crude clubs, one slashed with a hunting knife, and one fired a pistol, downing two soldiers.

Other guards fired back with rifles and pistols, killing all four attackers.

The uninjured looters scattered and ran. Colonel Bothwell shouted orders to his men, "Keep going! Keep going!"

The wagon drivers calmed their horses and forged ahead to the depot and presidential train.

The first wagon comes alongside the Treasury car, and the seemingly calm Colonel Bothwell steps across into the car.

Byron asks, "Are you all right?"

"Yes. Some men are dead. We have the assets. Now let's get on with it."

He turns to the lead guard, "Send two men back—take care of our downed men."

Guards take turns transferring the treasury assets; Bothwell checks each bag and each box which he had tagged the day before.

Rugerman double checks the action. When all items on the inventory list have been confirmed, Bothwell puts the list into his inner coat pocket. He waves the wagons away and orders the wagon train lead officers to stay in the depot and help guard the train.

On the adjoining track is the ambulance train. Some wounded and sick are already on board. Medics and soldiers help men on crutches while others wait to board.

Byron tells Ambrose, "Now I'll go talk to the Lynchburg conductor. David says we might know him."

He strides alongside the ambulance train until he sees the conductor looking up into the cab, talking to the engineer. The fireman shuts the boiler door and steps back, chucking his shovel aside. Byron grabs the hand hold as if to board the cab.

"Whoa!" says the conductor. "Who are you? You can't get on this train!"

Byron savors the warmth from the boiler door. "Excuse me. I have important government business. You know me and my brother, from Lynchburg." He pulls off his hat and goes on, "You must have seen him around here a few moments ago. Before the war, we used to bring you coffee. Aren't you Mr. Clay?"

"Yes. I'm Geoffrey Clay. Sure, the boy with the smooth face: I remember him. You look familiar, too, yes. But you can't ride here. Now get off."

"Yes, of course. I know you've got a lot of soldiers who need medical help. How many of these trips have you made in the last week?"

"So far, three. But from what I see and hear, this may be the last one. Never mind that. Get away."

"Yes, in a minute. What do you mean, Mr. Clay, 'The last one?'"

"Before we could get back here, this place will be full of Yankees. They already closed off the line from Petersburg. Look, we're about to leave. You can't hitch a ride here, even if I know you and you are an officer."

"I understand. After you leave Lynchburg, what are you going to do?"

"We'll deliver these medical cases, then I don't know. I may head on home to Salem, or just stay in Lynchburg."

"How is it to the west?"

"I've heard that Tennessee is shut off. But they say Salem may still be open. "

"What's the situation in Lynchburg?"

"It's not as bad as here, but it's not good even though it is still free. Now and then a small raid, on the outskirts. It's all dark at night; the streets are empty, except for one or two armed men here and there. Oil is dear, and even wood is costly. Home defense is old men and women. Able men are away at the front."

"What about daytime?"

"Some businesses are open, but they don't have much to sell. Most of the food coming in is immediately shipped on to the troops. But now that Petersburg is blocked off, who knows."

"There are thousands of wounded in hospitals. They're using hundreds of slaves as attendants, helping the nurses and doctors." Clay continues, "Each trip, maybe two or three of the wounded die even before we get there. At Lynchburg, they take them off, wrap them up, and go right to the cemetery."

Byron offers encouragement, "You've made a big difference to a lot of people, I've heard that. You've saved a lot of lives."

The crew nods, glad that someone appreciates them.

"I know you have to go—and I don't want to slow you down—but I need your help. In a different way. "

Clay wonders, "Like how?"

Byron surprises himself with how easily he spins an untrue story. "Here's the situation. We're shipping the remains of my wife's kid brother and a kin of Mrs. Davis to Ironville. We have other bodies for the same destination. There's an old car standing by. If I get the rest of the coffins aboard, I want to hook the car behind your train so it can at least get to Lynchburg. From there we'll either get a wagon or reload the coffins to hitch a ride on a V&T train headed west."

"I lost a brother-in-law. I know. I'm listening." Clay pauses briefly, then briskly resumes, "We'll be going after we're full, maybe an hour. Then this train is leaving. Is that all you want?"

"Yes sir. I know that you need to get away from the city as soon as possible. I don't have all the coffins this minute. They are on the way, just not at the depot yet. But the car should be here soon."

Clay responds, "We can't wait long. I have sick and wounded men here. They need medical help badly.'

"I understand. If I can't get the car coupled onto you within an hour, go ahead without me. But, if that happens, maybe you can still help anyway."

"How?

"You switch at Burkeville, don't you, Mr. Clay?"

"Yes. In fact we used to pick up cars of wounded there from Petersburg, before they got cut off. So?"

"That's still a safe area. No Yankees there now, and probably won't be any for at least another 24 hours. I'm asking that you wait just an hour or two, not here but there, at Burkeville." He gestures toward the presidential train. "Let me show you something." Byron leads Clay a few steps back, out of earshot of the engineer and fireman, and points to the presidential car.

"That one there is President Davis's train. It's heading for Danville after you leave. I could hook on to that, catch up with you at Burkeville and then cut loose."

"That's a big if. What if we wait two hours and you don't show up?"

"Then you just go ahead without me."

With his back to the engineer, Byron reaches in his pocket and draws out two eagle coins. He hands the conductor one. "Here's something for waiting. When I catch up, you'll get the other."

With new interest, Clay says, "I do have to stop at Burkeville, to get water and then switch over. I suppose an hour or two there won't hurt. There's no rush to make a roundtrip back to Richmond anyway. This is the last hospital train out of here this week, this year, maybe ever. All right. But you have to do the switches and the coupling. Not us."

"Agreed. I know how to do that. And I have a strong helper. I will only need you to back up. Two of us couldn't push the car to you."

"Fair enough. I'll wait two hours for you there. No more. And if there's any Yankee trouble, we won't wait at all."

Byron reaches for the conductor's firm hand. As they grip each other, Byron smiles, "So be it. You are indeed a gentleman. I thank you for your kindness. Good luck. I'll see you in Burkeville. And I'll have your other eagle."

"And good luck to you and your family, sir."

"One more thing. Once we get to Lynchburg, we'll need to have a way to go on and reach Ironville. Is there a depot stop there?"

"No. The closest would be Buford's."

"Buford's? Well, then, we'll need a way to get to Buford's. Start thinking how we could either tow our car or send the coffins there from Lynchburg."

"Maybe."

"We would pay fair cost to do that. I'll pay. I'll see you in Lynchburg." Byron strides away.

# CHAPTER 5

## *Aboard*

At the presidential train, its conductor and his engineer stand together near Davis's car. Byron looks at the conductor and says, "You sure have an important job tonight. What I need you to do for me is so minor, I almost hate to bring it up."

"What's that?"

"What's your name, sir?"

"Reed, Timothy Reed."

"Good to meet you, Mr. Reed. You see that old baggage car on the tail end there?"

Byron finds it is easier this time to spell out the cover story, "It's empty except for the bodies of some Lynchburg officers we're shipping home. We need to cut that car loose at Burkeville." He muddles the story by adding, "We'll be taking on other coffins there from Petersburg."

Reed asks, "And what do want us to do? We've got to get President Davis to Danville. That's our utmost priority."

"When you stop at Burkeville to check the crossover switch and take on water, just give us a minute or two to uncouple that car."

"And then what?"

"We'll hitch on to a passing train or take a wagon from there."

"That sounds simple enough."

He looks at the engineer. "What is your name, sir…and your home town?"

"William Alexander Prescott, sir. From Charleston."

"Glad to meet you. You gentlemen will be doing the right thing for the families. For them, I thank you."

"Are you authorized to do this?" asks Reed.

"Of course. I'm on the Cabinet staff. We're doing this on orders from some very senior officers. I assure you it's OK."

"Then I guess it's OK by me. Just don't slow us down when we leave Burkville. Decouple fast and get it over with."

"Understood."

And with that, Byron strides back toward the baggage cars. He sees a frail woman, carrying a sickly girl of about two, break through the line and attempt to board the last car. She pleads, "You have room. Take us with you! Please!"

She puts her little girl through the door and tries to climb up herself. But Caleb is there and hands the child back. "No, ma'am. Sorry. We can't. No. I'm sorry. NO!"

He shoves them away and thinks to himself, "Oh my God. She even looks like my Eliza!"

"You've got to take us! We can't stay here. We have no way to get out! Please!"

She turns to Byron, "Please, sir. Please let us on."

Byron bows his head and shoulders her aside. "Sorry, ma'am. Not on this train." Then, "Just a minute. Come with me."

He walks over to one of the guards. "Sergeant! See that this lady and her child are cared for." He notes the man's name and says to her, "You will be all right." He leaves her there with an incomplete sense of satisfaction.

Returning to the baggage car, Byron looks in the door and sees two pine coffins. "Good."

He tells Caleb, "Both conductors say they will help. What we need this train to do is easier than what we need the ambulance train to do."

"Can we trust them?"

"I think so. They seem like honorable men. David was right. I do know the the ambulance conductor—from long ago—Geoffrey Clay. I made sure he has some extra incentive: an eagle now, and another if he waits for us."

Caleb kneels down and holds the lantern near one of the coffins. "David got them here about an hour ago. They look like the real thing and smell like the real thing. On the lids there is even some lime spread around, as they do for preservation."

"David did well," says Byron. "He always does. He never lets me down. He concentrates on the details. When he is given an assignment, you know he will come through."

"David told me that the wagon driver asked who was in those caskets," responds Caleb. "He told them that they were high ranking officers who had died on the outskirts of Richmond and were dispatched to Lynchburg. He said one was his brother and the other was kin to Mrs. Davis. With his bald face and big eyes, he can be very believable. The driver accepted that."

"But why do they smell so bad?"

"Dead cats inside." Caleb reminds him, "That was planned."

"Poor cats. Probably starved to death."

"The tags say Lynchburg and have names no one would recognize." Byron reaffirms, "If anyone on this train sees the coffins, we want them to remember these names. I have different tags we'll put on at the right time. You stay here, Caleb, I'll go ahead and tell Ambrose that we are on plan."

Bothwell hears him out. He then directs David to go forward and report to Secretary Trenholm that all assets are aboard and that the team is ready.

David finds the Secretary in the front car, the only one with a wood stove for warmth. Mrs. Trenholm sits backward, facing her husband, who is studying the ambulance train as it begins to move out. Daughter Mary Jo, 19, is next to her father and on the aisle.

David bends forward. "Excuse me, Miss, I have a message for Secretary Trenholm." She leans back and gets her father, still seated, to turn around to face the aisle. Seeing David, Trenholm stands and leans toward him.

David whispers his message. Trenholm nods. David straightens up, and the Secretary returns to his seat.

Mary Jo gently touches David's arm, looks up, smiles, and says, "Father told me that you men are doing something extremely important. We thank you. Are you coming with us?"

"Yes, in another car."

"Maybe you can see me in Danville?"

"Maybe." He glances at her father, who is preoccupied looking out the window. He salutes him anyway and hurries out to rejoin the treasury team.

Finally President Davis arrives at the depot, escorted by aides on each side. He marches purposefully to the forward car, nodding briskly left and right at soldiers along the way. He mounts the stairs and doesn't look back.

Reed waves his lantern for the engineer to see and then climbs aboard the back of the presidential car. Not withstanding all the guards, he feels it is his responsibility to deliver the President safely to Danville.

Up forward, the fireman throws more wood into the firebox to build up steam in the boiler. Behind and beside the train are loyal soldiers and home guard volunteers who stand ready to hold back unwanted passengers now and to repel any Yankees later.

On the locomotive's cowcatcher are three soldiers. In the center, underneath the headlamp, stands a rifleman. Seated on either side of him are the others, with rifles and pistols. These men will watch for logs or rock blockades on the track and shoot any Yankees they might see.

Each passenger car has six guards with pistols and rifles near the doors and windows. Two soldiers ride outside at the front and between the cars.

Seven naval officers who had been stranded in Richmond accept assignment to help assist the regular guards secure the train and protect the passengers.

Colonel Bothwell commandeers two of the young, pistol-bearing ensigns: one to help him guard the assets in the dimly lit Treasury car, where David Rugerman stares at the asset bags and boxes, and the other to help Byron Rugerman and Caleb Cornish defend the rear of the train.

One ensign waits for further direction from Bothwell. The other comes through the coffin car, looks down at the caskets and squints, able only to see "Lynchburg." He wrinkles his nose as he heads for the rear, where Byron instructs him to stand outside on the coupler.

It is almost midnight when the whistle blows. The four big drive wheels begin to turn and move the engine forward, snatching the slack between the cars with a clank, first one, and then another, and still another. Any sound of distant artillery is drowned out by the "whoosh whoosh" of the engine stack. The presidential train creeps out, carrying hopes for escape, for a new capitol, and for safety of the Cabinet and its treasury.

About ten minutes out, the drizzle stops and a gentle breeze disperses the mist and clears the skies, allowing the engineer to drive by moonlight reflected off the rails. The locomotive headlamp is extinguished. The train approaches full night speed.

Bothwell calls his men and the ensigns back together. "We are on our way. Next stop: Burkeville—about 4 hours. The engine will take on water there."

Byron asks, "Colonel, does that mean we should keep our same positions now?"

"Yes and no. The Federals may have small scouting parties probing or maybe worse. The threat now is not behind us, but ahead. We have to protect our people up front and be ready for any attempts to stop this train."

David inquires, "Where do you want us, sir?"

"David, you stay right here with me, guarding the treasury. Captain: you and the lieutenant move into the coffin car, to protect the backside of this car."

He looks at the ensigns and continues, "And you Navy gentlemen, I want you both outside in front of this car, one on each side. There should be none of our people along the tracks. Be ready to shoot any Yankee you might see. The moon will help, and a little light spills out of the cars ahead. Keep watch for campfires, or the flash of gunfire. Don't wait for them to shoot you first."

The ensigns step out the front door of the treasury car. Byron locks it. Now there is only the four man treasury team. Ambrose reviews the plan. "We rendezvous with the ambulance train at Burkeville. David, when did that train leave Richmond?"

"Less than an hour before we did, maybe 45 minutes. I sure hope it waits for us."

Ambrose soberly comments, "It better. Or we're going to have to come up with a miracle."

David worries, "And I hope we don't run into any Yankees. If you miss that ambulance train, the whole plan will fall apart. If you have to round up wagons to haul those coffins, that wouldn't be much help. You could never outrun Federal cavalry men. We need that train."

Byron solemnly replies, "I trust Mr. Clay."

Ambrose says, with clenched teeth, "David, never mind 'what ifs'. At this moment, right here, right now. There is work to be done here, in this train, now. "

"And quick," notes Caleb.

Up ahead, at the front of the train, three soldiers on the cowcatcher watch for trouble, their eyes adjusted to the moon-lit terrain. The center man focuses directly ahead, struggling against the monotony of the shiny rails and blurry, steady stream of approaching railroad ties. The other men scan each side ahead, fixing now and then on approaching groves of trees or piles of rocks which might hide snipers. Guns cocked, they are ready to defend the President, his staff, and the treasury.

In the President's car, at each end, in spite of the chilly weather, some windows are open, where soldiers sit, resting their rifles on the sills. They, too, are ready.

And farther back, the Navy men and the Ambrose team stay alert. They need to be.


A few miles ahead, three grim-faced Yankees wearing dark hats are stealthily trudging northwest through Chesterfield County. They are Sergeant Howard Mann, a Marylander, and Privates Richard Stringer and James Chapin from Connecticut. Out of uniform, they know that if they were to be captured, they would be shot as spies. Their mission is to gather infor-mation about Confederate railroads and troop movements. Though they are spies, they are prepared for serious fighting, too. Each carries the radical Spencer 7-shot .52 caliber repeat-er rifle, with extra rounds stuffed in their coat pockets.

They discover railroad tracks ahead, perpendicular to their path.

Mann, barely audible, says, "All right. We've found the tracks. These appear intact. We're supposed to check a mile each way and report back to the colonel. I'll go south a mile. You two go north. Then we meet again here. Let's go. Now."

# CHAPTER 6

## *Ambush*

In the Treasury car, Ambrose exhales and announces, "Step one is done. We're out of Richmond. Now we do step two."

All four of them know the plan and how they will divide up the treasury assets. The carefully chosen reserve will be removed from the Treasury car, and redirected for storage west of Lynchburg. The remainder, most of the assets, will continue on to Danville.

Caleb and David enter the coffin car. It seems to rattle more than the one they just left. There are no heavy Treasury bags on the floor to dull the noises and no car behind it to dampen the swaying of the rear.

As David lowers a lantern nearby, Caleb pulls his trusty hunting knife from his boot and pries open the coffin lids.

"I put some empty sacks in each one," says David.

Though he knows what to expect, Caleb makes a face and shakes his head at the sight of the dead cats. He drops the lids on the floor and lifts out the empty bags. He and David return to the Treasury car.

Bothwell, who supervised the count at Richmond, pulls out a small list of paper, squats down and opens a bag full of coins. "Let's get started." In his concentration, he is oblivious to the noises and rattles of the train. But outside, trouble is brewing.

After a few hundred yards, Yankee Stringer stops, and calls, "Wait. Hear that? One's coming! Sounds like a mile or so away. It could get here in a few minutes."

Now Mann hears it too: a rumbling noise. "We should try to stop it."

Chapin says, "How could we derail it? There are no rocks or logs around here, and we have no explosives."

"Still, we should try to stop it. Or at least slow it down. We'll have to shoot. Puncture the boiler or get the engineer. They surely have guards on it—a lot more than the three of us. But we have the advantage: surprise. We take our shots and fall back. Before they can shoot back or stop the train to come after us, we make a quick getaway. It's worth a try."

"There," points Stringer, "there's a rise near the track. If we lie down up there we'll have a good angle and they won't see us."

Mann cautions, "They'll be moving right along. We won't get many chances. We should first aim for the middle of the boiler, and our next rounds go for the engineer. We'd be about eye level with him."

"Will our Spencers make holes in the boiler?"

"If we hit it square, so it doesn't ricochet... there's a chance. Of course it would be a while before the steam loss would cause the train to slow down."

They scurry to the top of the rise and lie prone—Stringer on the left, Mann and Chapin to his right—behind some bushes. They load and cock their rifles. Each pulls out some extra rounds to hold in his right hand.

"All right," says Mann, "Pan as they get near. First shot is the middle of the boiler. Second shot is the engineer, and follow up at anyone you see in cars. Don't fire until I do, but then fire right way and keep firing. Let's each take three shots and then fall back."

40

The rumbling is now enriched by a wheezing and some clunking. The train lumbers toward their position. Guns at the front. Guns sticking out of cars.

"Oh my God! Look at all that firepower!" exclaims Chapin.

"Ignore those guys up front. Shoot for the boiler, then the engineer. Ready?"

Mann fires. A fraction of a second later, Stringer fires. Then Chapin. As the cab passes by, Mann fires at the engineer. Stringer and Chapin follow suit.

Inside the train, passengers and crew hear gunfire. Ambrose barks, "Yankees!" David freezes.

Byron and Caleb dive to the floor, simultaneously pulling out and cocking their pistols.

Dull pops, from up front on the left, east side. Seconds later, many shots, louder than the first.

Then a single, louder pop just ahead of the Treasury car. They hear a crack as a bullet splinters the wall of their car. Ambrose grunts and grabs his left wrist. "I'm hit!"

Outside, up ahead on the cowcatcher, the front left soldier saw the flash of Mann's shot and swung his rifle around. After the second Yankee shot, front left found the ambush spot and drew a bead. He fired.

Mann's shot at the engineer again gave away his position. The front gunner of the president's car tracked the three Federal flashes and he popped a round at the spot. A soldier at the rear of the President's car fired, too.

After the Yankees had each fired twice, a hail of lead came their way. The engine nose gunner got off a second shot. The Davis car guards fired three times.

As the Treasury car passed the Federals' position, Davis's guards fired two more at the spot. Mann and Stringer died instantly from head wounds. Chapin is mortally wounded in the neck, but managed to get off one more shot as the coffin car passed by. Then the Federals were silent.

It all lasted about ten seconds. The Federals had fired seven times. The defenders fired nine rounds. The boiler survives. The engineer is unhurt. But his fireman took a bullet in his thigh, causing him to crumble in pain. Ambrose Bothwell's left hand is covered with blood.

The train continues toward Danville, leaving behind traces of gun smoke over the spot where Mann, Stringer and Chapin lay dead. When the nose soldiers look back, they see the engineer waving for help. One soldier works his way aft to the cab, inching along the walk strip next to the boiler; he will fill in for the fireman.

David rigidly stares at Bothwell's hand. "Blood. You're bleeding. Your hand has blood all over. Look at the blood."

The Colonel straightens to full height, holds his left hand to his chest, and responds, "I'll be all right. Just a surface wound." He looks at David and points to the forward door. "Find out what happened."

David steps forward and cautiously unlatches the front door. An ensign is there, staring intently down and away from the train. David asks, "What was that?"

"It was Yankees. But I guess they missed. I really couldn't see. Our men must have gotten them. I shot at a lump we passed by. That must have been them."

The other Navy man says, "I couldn't see anything from my side. It all happened fast."

"Good job. If word comes back," replies David, "knock on the door. But for now, keep watching." David locks the door. The four treasury comrades gather again in the center of the car. David pulls a lantern close. Byron and Caleb return their pistols to their holsters.

"Is that it?" asks David.

The routine rumble of the train is his answer.

# CHAPTER 7

## *Division*

With his right hand, Ambrose Bothwell begins pulling rolls of eagles from a bag and says, "We have work to do." Byron holds open one of the smelly bags; Ambrose drops in forty rolls. "That's enough. Caleb, let's have the next one."

Byron ties his bag and discovers that he needs both hands to lift it. He heads to the coffin car, thinking, "It didn't look that heavy."

When Caleb's first bag is ready, Ambrose reminds him, "Put that in a different coffin. You and Captain Rugerman alternate, so we divide the weight up."

Byron and Caleb go back and forth until they have achieved their goal, 350 pounds of assets (about 4,200 troy ounces), worth the then-enormous sum of $84,000.

After filling the last coin bag, Bothwell reaches into the special Treasury sack containing jewelry which had been donated by southern ladies. He comes up with a pearl necklace and a handful of gold pins, rings and jeweled earrings. David moves the lantern closer, and Ambrose holds out his hand for all to see. "This must be very valuable. It represents much sacrifice. My own mother gave some family heirlooms. Even a pair of her grandmother's earrings, not unlike these."

None of these men know much about jewelry, but all are impressed. Byron quietly comments, "Some day I hope I can buy something really nice like that for Eliza."

Ambrose Bothwell interrupts. "Some of this can go to Danville, but we will put half of it where it will be safe, in the reserve. Captain, Byron, put this bag in Charles's coffin."

Ambrose checks his list. "Caleb, put the lids back on those coffins. Smear some of the lime around, too. And give me a little of that lime for my wrist."

The four gather again, and Bothwell reminds them that Secretary Paulson told them to carry money to buy what they might need to get the job done. "Byron. Caleb. Here, take these." There are two rolls. Each gets one.

Caleb hitches up his pants and tightens his belt. "I feel like a rich man!"

Byron tightens his belt and pats his bulging pocket. "It's not ours. We have part of the Confederacy in our pockets."

Ambrose checks his list of what assets were transferred to the reserve. He retrieves the original Treasury audit list he used when the wagons delivered the assets to the train. Then, from a breast pocket, he unfolds still a third list. That will be the new 'official' audit list. He carefully compares the three lists. Satisfied, he hands the transferred assets list to Byron.

"Byron, Captain, fold that up. Keep it on you. That's the count of the reserve, what's in the coffins. Not on the list is what's in your pockets."

He holds up the third list. "And now, we each need to sign this new 'official' list of assets, those that go to Danville. This is what goes in the record books." Ambrose pencils at the top "CSA Treasury Assets 2 April 1865 Richmond." At the bottom, with a flourish, he writes. "Attest," and then, below, "Ambrose Bothwell, Col., Auditor." Under that he writes "Witnesseth." Byron, Caleb and David each pencil their signatures. Ambrose carefully folds it, puts it in his breast pocket, and steps into a clear area of the car.

"Byron, give me the old coffin tags. David, bring that lantern over here." He ceremoniously crinkles them and the original list of treasury assets and, setting them on fire, drops them to the floor.

The feeble flames flare and die out. Caleb is fascinated. With a sigh of accomplishment, Colonel Ambrose Bothwell, Colonel of the Confederate States of America, a living symbol of responsibility and serious demeanor, breaks into a broad boyish grin. Caleb thinks, "I didn't think he ever smiled! Very few people had ever seen him look like that."

Regathering his composure, Colonel Bothwell quietly proclaims, "Step two. Completed. They only scratched me. See?" he holds up his left hand. "The bleeding has stopped. We are doing all right. Thank you, gentlemen."

David comes forth and, with an original jittering, sliding step, mixes dust and dirt with the ashes until the floor shows no evidence of paper or fire.

The smell of burned paper dissipates as Byron again reviews what is planned next. The team will go separate ways at Burkeville: two for Danville, two for the West.

Ambrose asks Byron, "Captain, do you really know how to uncouple that car?"

"Yes. I haven't ever actually done it, but I watched the yard men do it many times at Lynchburg. Caleb and I will do it just fine."

"Get the ensigns back in here," Ambrose points to David.

"Gentlemen. Welcome back inside. We are now in safe Confederate territory. You ensigns will now help me and Lieutenant David Rugerman protect the Treasury the rest of the way to Danville. You two men," he nods stiffly towards Byron and Caleb, "Captain, Lieutenant, we will be leaving you at our next stop. Thank you for helping guard our valuable assets. Good luck on your sad mission. Perhaps we may meet again some day."

Byron formally responds, "You are welcome, Colonel, sir. After we deliver the bodies to Lynchburg, we will join with defense forces there. God speed to you all." They salute each other.

Byron and Caleb reenter the coffin car. Byron checks his pocket watch. "We have about two hours before Burkeville. Let's rest while we can. You nap. I'll wake you when it's my turn."

# CHAPTER 8

# *Coupling*

After uncertain days at Richmond, after the attack ambush, and after transferring the assets, this is a welcome lull. For the first time Byron and Caleb can be fully aware of the train's motion and noises: rumbling and rattling and wobbling. Up front, passengers are sleeping at last, relieved to be out of Richmond and past the firefight and lulled by the warmth of the wood stove. The quarter moon seems higher, brighter, illuminating the countryside passing by.

Once again, Byron switches name tags on the coffins. "Ironville" now replaces "Lynchburg." That task finished, he stares out the door. The pure wood smoke left by the engine reminds him of the fireplace at home. Not like the acrid fumes permeating Richmond. Caleb curls up on the floor next to the coffins and quickly falls asleep.

Byron continues to fret, asking himself, "Will that ambulance train be waiting for us in Burkeville? Conductor Clay seemed trustworthy to me. If he's not there, we're in serious trouble. I have to assume that he will be there. Right now there's nothing we can do about it one way or the other. I'm glad Caleb is here. I trust him—and he's such an energetic guy."

The train rumbles on. About half an hour elapses.

"Caleb, wake up! It's my turn." Caleb stretches, rubs his eyes, and stands up, swaying a little with the train's wobbling. "I could have slept a lot longer." Yawn. "Your turn."

Byron chooses to rest against the west side of the car, believing that any new Yankee bullets would come from the east side.

Caleb stands at the doors, occasionally leaning out and looking ahead. The fresh moist night air helps to clear his sleep sodden mind. He glances back at his brother-in-law. He shakes his head thinking, "It didn't take him long to go to sleep. I sure hope that train is there when we get there. If it's not, we're going to have to find some other way. But even if it's not there, we're going to have to cut loose from the President's train. We'll be on our own."

"Byron, wake up. We're slowing down. We must be near Burkeville."

Byron pulls out his pocket watch and nods. "It's about time. It seems a little brighter than when we left Richmond. The sun will be up in a while. Are you ready to uncouple? We must do it pretty speedy. Soon as this thing stops."

He scans the area. "I don't see the other train over there. It's there somewhere. As soon as we stop, we'll both get out of here quick and uncouple. I'll show you what to do."

The train squeaks to a clunking halt. Up front, Conductor Timothy Reed sends guards ahead to check the crossover switch, grab the lever and throw it so the President's train can continue straight ahead. Guards carry the wounded fireman back to the second passenger car where he can get medical attention.

Caleb and Byron move to the coupler.

Inside the passenger cars, most are still sleep. From the back of the Treasury car, David looks down and watches Byron and Caleb wrestling with the heavy coupler. They struggle, they grab, they twist, they lean left and right. David has faith in brother Byron who saw this task done many times at the Lynchburg rail yard.

Byron and Caleb pull the pins and release the links, then stand up and nod at David. David holds up three fingers and mouths toward them, "Step three!"

Conductor Reed sees Byron take a deep breath and give a thumbs up. Just moments later the train begins to creep away.

Bothwell has been watching, too, wondering, "Where is that Lynchburg train? I don't see it. Is this the end of our plan?"

The government train chugs away towards Danville, pulling the Treasury baggage car carrying David and Ambrose, who will vouch for the integrity of "the" Treasury assets. Colonel Ambrose Bothwell leans out and waves a salute to Captain Byron Rugerman and Lieutenant Caleb Cornish whom he leaves behind. They do not see him.

At Burkeville, it now seems too quiet. The coffin car sits there, quietly, except for an occasional squeak or creek as it relaxes. Byron feels his gut tighten up. He thinks, "Here we are—with all that money. Just my brother-in-law and me and two side arms. We would have a tough time fighting off a crowd of robbers or Yankees."

Aloud he says, "I don't see the train. It must be here. Where could we even find a wagon here? There's nobody here! It's got to be here. I'm sure I could trust that Clay. Caleb, go look down that Lynchburg track."

Caleb starts trotting along the tracks heading west. With heart pounding, he paces himself to avoid tripping on the railroad ties.

Then, in the predawn moonlight he sees, around a curve, hundreds of yards from the crossover, a dark form on the tracks ahead. He breaks into a run, still stepping only on the ties. Yes, it is indeed the train. He yells back at Byron "Yes! He's here! Yes!" He reaches the dimly lit last ambulance car.

There paces Geoffrey Clay looking at his watch. He extends his hand. "We were expecting you. We saw your train. Where's the Captain?"

Byron comes running and says, "Thanks for waiting for us. Bless you. I'm glad to see you. Why are you way over here?"

"We didn't want any Federals to see us near that main line. They may be coming from the east, through Dinwiddie—following the Southside tracks. We heard a train—and are glad that it is you. We're ready to go. We've got to go. We'll get you to Lynchburg for sure. We'll back up but you've got to reset the switch first. We'll bump you and you hook on."

Byron responds, "I knew you were a man of your word. Yeah, we'll set the switch. Start backing up and we'll let you know when you're close to the coupler."

Clay waves to the engineer, who also is anxious to move on. He orders the fireman to throw in more logs and opens the draft to build more steam pressure. Clay climbs into the last ambulance car.

Byron and Caleb race back to the crossover and push over the switch lever. Byron says, "I'll go back to our car coupler. You let me know when he's about fifty feet away." Caleb runs toward the ambulance train and gestures it backwards. The train slowly rumbles through the switch with Caleb jogging alongside.

Hooking up to the coupler is not as easy as they had expected. The slots are a mismatch. But not too much for two strong young men. They use the pins as levers to raise and lower the links and nudge the slots into line. At last the pins lock in.

Byron is on the right, or west, side and Caleb on the left. Byron waves ahead to the conductor. Almost immediately, the engine puffs and pulls, and like links in a chain the cars start to follow.

Meanwhile, a Federal scout has been plodding westward parallel to the Petersburg tracks toward Burkeville. He sees the train and spots the two Confederate officers. One of them, Byron, disappears when he readies to enter the car on the far side. The scout has no time to backtrack a quarter mile to his unit. He pulls up his rifle and jogs forward a few paces. When about 900 feet away, he hastily fires at Caleb. There is a bang and, almost simultaneously, a buzz and a thud as a bullet smacks into the back of the car near Caleb's head. The scout reloads. Caleb whirls, drops into a crouch, and raises his pistol. Holding it with both hands and elbows straight, he points it in the direction of the fired shot. The moon reflects off the Federal's rifle. Caleb sees the flash of the second rifle shot and fires back with three quick rounds. The scout huffs, grunts, and falls to the ground, moaning.

As the train rolls forward, Byron calls out, "Get in. Get in!" Caleb pulls himself up into the coffin car.

"Did you get him?"

"I think so."

"Is he dead?"

"I don't know. I just wanted to stop him shooting at us. He could have killed me!"

"Forget him. His unit will be along soon—we can't wait to find out."

Byron then works his way forward to consult with Clay.

Clay asks, "What was that all about? Are you all right? Are they coming after us?"

"One Yankee only. Probably dead now. I didn't see any others. I think we're in the clear. Have you got any more ideas how we can take our bodies on to Ironville?"

"Yes, with luck, it's possible. At the Lynchburg yard, we could probably put you on a Virginia-Tennesse towards Salem.

They don't stop in Ironville. The nearest is Buford's. You'd have to get off there."

Byron affirms, "Understood. We could probably get some farmer to haul us on to Ironville. We'll unload the coffins in Lynchburg and count on you to help get us on board a V&T. Any boxcar going west would do."

Clay answers, "It may take an hour or several hours. Nobody is keeping much of a schedule. But I do have friends there."

Byron answers, "I'm sure. You've been a real friend to us, too. Oh, of course—here is the other coin I promised. And there will be another one once we are on the Virginia-Tennesse train." They shake hands.

Byron rejoins Caleb, where—unknown to anyone else on the ambulance train—almost a fifth of a ton of Confederate Treasury assets is en route for safekeeping near Buford's.

Caleb sighs, "God willing, next stop, Lynchburg."

Byron adds, "I want to see my parents, yet it's best we just hurry through."

Later, six of Sheridan's cavalry pull up at the Burkeville crossing.

No people. No train. One dead scout.

# CHAPTER 9

# *Westward*

The men alternate napping as the train rolls towards Lynchburg.

Lynchburg had escaped being the scene of serious battles. Its buildings are intact and its rail yard still functions. Virtually all able men are off to battle. With railroad tracks coming in from north, south, east and west, it became a hospital oasis, accepting wounded and sick from all directions. Indeed, thousands of patients were housed in makeshift hospitals, with a handful of doctors, scores of women nurse volunteers, and hundreds of slave attendants.

Now, though the sun is shining, the mood of this unscathed place is dark and sad. At the rail yard, the engineer locks his brakes, chokes the fire, and sets the bypass.

Byron commandeers a cart. He and Caleb slide the caskets out of the baggage car, and Byron says, "You guard the cart. I'll line up the next move and find something to eat. I'll talk with Mr. Clay."

He walks past the train as some of the wounded are being helped out. Wagons stand ready to take the immobiles to the hospitals. Ambulance trains often lose two, three or more patients who die before arrival. Duiguid undertaker personnel are waiting with wagons. Thousands of war casualties—from the field, from the hospitals—men from Virginia and far away states—have already been interred in Lynchburg.

Byron catches up to conductor Geoffrey Clay and reminds him, "I'm counting on you to get us a ride."

Clay replies, "Stay here. I'll be back in a few minutes."

Byron watches him walk across nearby tracks and thinks, "He came through for us once, we need him now. If he doesn't get us a tow or a ride, I'll have to get my family involved in this thing some way. They might get us a wagon and horses. Much as I love my family, I really don't want more people to know what we're doing." His mind eases a bit when he sees the conductor briskly return.

Clay takes hold of his shoulder and leads him back across the tracks toward another track where stands another train with locomotive idly wheezing.

"Looks like you're in luck. Virginia-Tennesse is making up a western train. I think I can get you on it. You stand here. Let me handle it."

Byron finds a vendor and buys a big baked roll and an unstopped flask of dubious water. He tears off half the roll, stuffs it in his mouth, and gulps half of the water.

A couple of minutes later conductor Clay returns and says, "He'll do it. He stops at Buford's, so then you have to get yourself to Ironville. He'll let you put your bodies in that last boxcar over there. Number 84. Just in front of the caboose. There. Do it quick. He's says he's leaving in half an hour. His name is Richard Lancaster. I had to give him my eagles. Reimburse me please. Now. Then I'll introduce you."

Byron pulls out more coins and hands them to conductor Clay. They step over to the V&T train. Clay introduces Lancaster and says, "I have to take care of my business. I'll see you again sometime when this is all over."

Byron tells Lancaster the story of his mission, detailing that Mrs. Davis's nephew died in the Chimborazo hospital, as did cousin Albert. "We promised to get the bodies to Ironville. What's it like out west from here?"

"It was all right yesterday," replies Lancaster, "but I don't get good information about where the Yankees are. It'll be dark when I drop you off at Buford's. How quickly can you get your coffins into boxcar 84?"

"Just a few minutes. My lieutenant and I will roll the cart over."

"Well, do it."

Byron trots away, careful not to spill the water, relieved that he has got the ride—and pleased that he hadn't given his name to Lancaster.

He looks for Caleb and is startled to see that the cart isn't there.

Caleb had been resting, hunched against a yard marker post, and was now asleep. Byron interrupts his nap with a shout, "Where's the cart?"

Caleb jumps up and they both start scanning the yard. Caleb spots it a few hundred feet away, being pushed somberly by two black men.

"There it is! Whoa, whoa, stop!" yells Caleb.

They ignore the call and keep going.

Byron and Caleb run after them. "Stop, stop right now!" yells Byron.

"Now!" yells Caleb commandingly.

The cart men stop and turn. "We're with Duiguid's. We meet every train. We take care of these things. We do it all right."

"No, no, these are not for Lynchburg. We're taking them to Ironville," says Caleb.

Byron adds warmly, "You all have a difficult job—you have been doing a good job—a tough job. But as an officer, I assure you that you do not have to bury these two bodies here in Lynchburg. They are going to relatives of Mrs. Davis in

Ironville. Now, can you help us please? Into box car 84 over there? Thank you, gentlemen."

That done, Caleb wolfs down his half roll and savors his share of the water. Byron trots over to the telegraph office and sends his memorized, meaningful wire to Eliza. He looks up towards the city and visualizes his mother and father. "Hello, father. Hello, mother," he whispers. He salutes, turns away, strides to the V&T train, and climbs up into boxcar 84.


It is late afternoon when the five-car Virginia & Tennesse train pulls out. Byron, Caleb and two coffins share space in the last box car with some nondescript crates. The men sit on the floor, facing each other.

The train clears the city, rolling on the old rail roadbed that first served Lynchburg in 1852. Their car wobbles left and right, and lurches (more left than right) as it follows around the Blackwater Marsh and heads for Liberty, Thaxton Switch, Buford's, Big Lick, Salem, and towards Bristol. They pass Forest Depot which had been the destination of Lynchburg's first railroad excursion.

Onward they roll more smoothly towards Liberty. David's report of a week ago was correct; Bedford County home folks had done well in replacing the section of tracks which General Hunter's people had torn up last year.

Caleb yawns and says, "It will be mighty good to see Father, Sister and the Farm."

Byron stretches his arms and says, "I want to see my kids. Mostly I want to see Eliza. When you have a wife, you'll understand. I miss her more than you can know."

Caleb seems lost in his thoughts. He stares at his feet. "I miss that farm. It was my whole life. When this war is over, I want to be back on the farm—to stay. Nobody is getting killed on the farm. We only hunt or kill to eat. There's been too much killing."

56

"I understand, Caleb. The farm is a fine place. It's good my children are there. They can learn a lot from their grandpa. But for me, Eliza is most important."

Caleb perks up and says, "Some day, I'll get married, like you. I've been thinking about it. There's a girl in Buford's who is really nice. Name is Hannah, Hannah Caldwell. A young friend of Eliza's. Some day I'll point her out. She's a farm girl." He pauses. "Byron, you know, that land has been in the family many, many years. Generations. Things were pretty good there when I was growing up. My father and uncle shared the original family tract. My mother, my sister, my brother and I could help them do what had to be done. Of course, our slaves, Ezekiel and Adam, did most of the hard work."

"Yeah."

"Since I left for the war, so much has changed. Mother and Brother are gone. The slaves are gone. Father and Sister can't get everything done. So much has happened while I've been gone." His voice trails off as his mind recalls bits and pieces of news that he'd received after leaving home.

# CHAPTER 10

## *Farm*

Every farm has a history, filled with joy, sadness, and even mystery.

Meadow Valley Farm, in Bedford County north of Buford's depot, is a 360-acre tract of meadow and grazing land which stretches gently from Goose Creek on up the valley to knolls and hills at the base of the Blue Ridge Mountains and the massive Peaks of Otter. The land had been patented with a grant from King George III in 1760 and has been in the Cornish family ever since. Some 120 acres were now farmed by Henry Cornish, a bachelor. The larger portion, 240 acres, now belongs to Francis Cornish, III, who lived with his wife, two sons, and two daughters in a century-old four-room house built of chestnut logs. It is a simple structure with a fireplace in the main room, a small room for the parents, another small room for the girls, and a loft-like attic where the boys sleep. A spring-fed stream brings clear water next to the house. Down the hill is the privy.

Just south of the Cornish farm is the small farm of the strange and reclusive Clinton Hallock who speaks rarely but watches often.

Henry Cornish, less enthusiastic about farming than brother Francis, had persuaded Francis to oversee his farm while he went to California to find gold and maybe a wife. After three years out west, Henry returned—without a wife but with a small, heavy pack. When anyone asked him if he found gold, he would say, "It was a fine experience. I came home richer than when I left." And then his face would slowly permit a cryptic smile.

His answer failed to squelch villager rumors that Henry Cornish had found gold.

Francis Cornish, III, 57, like so many farmers of rural Virginia, struggled after his sons went to war. His youngest son, Newton, had gone off to Virginia Military Institute while a teenager. Eldest son Caleb, then 22, joined the Confederate Army early in 1861 and was promoted to serve on the head-quarters staff in Richmond.

Oldest daughter, Katherine, is one of the "enemy," which doesn't alter her parents' love for her. She and her husband had ventured to Kentucky nearly a decade ago. Now he is in the Federal army, and she has enough to do taking care of her two children and tending her farm while her man is off to war.

Francis and his wife Anne were grateful when daughter Eliza came back to live with them after her husband, Byron, joined the Confederate Army in 1862.

Eliza is energetic and more physically fit than most women. Five and a half feet tall, with dark hair pulled back with a bow, she grew up on the farm, where she developed skills of home-making as well as farming.

She has strong inner strength, reinforced by her faith, and though not the eldest of the four children, she exhibited leader-ship even as a small girl, organizing family chores and events. More often than not, she subtly induces even her father to do what she has decided.

She learned her Bible well; she often cites passages appli-cable to family situations and problems. She takes on more re-sponsibilities than necessary and hesitates laughing at herself. She always seems to be in charge, except when older brother Caleb intervenes to save her from hurting herself when she tries something too strenuous.

She was just 19, but had parental blessing, when she married Byron Rugerman, a man she admired and adored. It was with mixed emotions when she left the farm back in 1859 to become a Lynchburg homemaker.

It made sense for her to be back with her parents on the farm with her small daughter while expecting the birth of another child in August. It made her happy to be really home. But she misses Byron, hungering for his love. Each new day seems too long since he went to war.

With the Cornish boys gone, Francis especially treasures the help of their middle-aged, but able, slave, Ezekiel, whom Francis inherited in 1836. Brother Henry's slave, Adam, worked with Ezekiel on crop land shared by the Cornish brothers. Henry Cornish himself helps on occasion, but without enthusiasm or commitment.

The slave brothers, Adam and Ezekiel, had been purchased at auction in Danville by Francis's father in 1825 when both were young. Their parents were West Indian and their classic features hint of Nigerian heritage. When the elder Francis died, he willed Ezekiel and 240 acres to son Francis, and to bachelor son Henry he willed Adam and 120 acres.

The slaves did the general labor, including raising and readying tobacco for market. They planted, cultivated, and harvested the sloping tobacco fields and shepherded the sheep in the pastures shared by the Cornish men. Ezekiel and Adam had acquired skill in shearing; the Cornishes rented out the slaves to shear neighbors' sheep. The Cornish families encouraged their slaves to attend church and learn the Bible, but they were reluctant to let them read much else which might stir up discontentment.

One fall day, Francis said, "Eliza, Ezekiel seems to be moving slow. I think he must be sick. Would you please go see if that's the case?"

Eliza sought out Ezekiel at the simple dirt-floored, one-room cabin he shared with Adam. He was sitting in the doorway, letting the sun warm away the chill in the air.

"How are you doing, Ezekiel? Father wonders if you are sick."

"Miss Eliza, ma'am, thank you. Yes, I'ze not been feel'n good for several days now."

"What seems to be the matter?"

"Well, ma'am, it's my stomach. I think I caught something from some of the other darkies at church on Sunday. There was talk of stomach pains goin' roun'."

"Are you eating and sleeping all right?"

"Well, Miss Eliza, I warn't. But now I is. I'ze tolerable better than I was. I don't think it's consumption."

"I'm glad. How is Adam?"

"He don' seem to have no trouble."

"That's good. We want you both to be well. Father wants you to take two or three days to just rest. There is plenty of peppermint in the herb garden. I would be glad to bring you some to ease your stomach. Would you like that?"

"Thank you kindly, Miss Eliza, but I'ze doing better. If I take a turn, I'll send Adam for some of dat mint. Thank you for coming to see 'bout me."

Back at the house, Eliza told her father that Ezekiel would take two or three days of rest. Her father nods, "Good. That's what I want. Henry and I take good care of our boys. Other than the farm itself, those boys are the most valuable property willed to us. We can't afford to lose either one of them."

Early in 1863, word filtered throughout the South that President Lincoln had issued an Emancipation Proclamation, declaring that all slaves everywhere in the country were to be free.

Francis fretted about how that could affect him and the Cornish farm. He thought, "We can barely get by now. How could we possibly manage without Ezekiel and Adam?"

Though Ezekiel considered Cornish to be a decent master, Ezekiel yearned to be his own man. Even if Master Francis died, it would be unlikely that Ezekiel would be willed his freedom. He was too important in the operation of the farm. And there was no way he could save up enough money to buy his freedom from the Cornishes. He was gray, but he was intelligent and still strong, and believed he could do better in life in freedom, up North.

Ezekiel and Adam sometimes talked about the idea of being on their own. They shared a dream of a better, though unknown, life.

Yet it always came down to trying to see how they could really get away without being hunted down and brought back like stray cattle.

Ezekiel believed Lincoln's Proclamation as offering real hope. He told Adam, "Maybe the North, the Federals, will come here and free us." Adam agrees, "Let's hope it will happen."

Francis and Henry were managing, but without Caleb and Newton to help, Francis postponed fixing a leak in the roof of his chestnut log barn or propping up the sagging wall of the shearing shed. Cornish fences would have to look good enough to fool the cattle and sheep because they could not stop the animals from wandering if they were very determined to do so.

He was thankful that Eliza was there. After caring for her two small children, she pitched in to help with the farm.

These were difficult times for the Cornishes; yet more serious trouble was on the way.

Francis was hit by two tragedies, two profound losses, one year after the other. Life for Francis became almost unbearable.

In May 1863, word came of the death of Newton at age 22. The report of his death was unclear and incomplete, as were most reports during the chaos of war. Where, when, how did it happen? Was it as a result of enemy action or some kind of infection or disease? Was that all they said? Didn't they know?

This much was said: Newton was with VMI cadets who were supporting Lt. Gen. Thomas ("Stonewall") Jackson northeast of Staunton. Shortly thereafter, Jackson himself was fatally wounded at Chancellorsville. This much was certain: Newton was dead, Jackson was dead.

Anne Cornish sank into deep depression at the loss of her "baby." When an epidemic of smallpox reached Bedford County, she became infected while helping tend a sick friend. Anne was unable or unwilling to fight it off.

Francis lost his love and helpmate, dead at 53. Francis asked himself, "What am I to do?" Here, at the beginning of that new grief, he must bury Anne.

Henry put together the simple box, and Ezekiel and Adam dug the hole in the family cemetery on the piney knoll above the barn. Eliza and Francis walked, hand in hand, to the cemetery. Henry began a prayer. Father and daughter prayed together and leaned on each other for what seemed like a lifetime. They would lean on each other more in the years ahead. Henry shoveled the first dirt. Ezekiel completed the job.

Eliza sobbed twice and Francis cried, "Goodbye my dearest love, my life."

Over time, Francis would increase his dependence on daughter Eliza, then 24.

There were other stones of sadness there: his mother's and father's, and two stones for Victoria, his first wife who died decades earlier during a painful still birth. Francis wondered where Newton's body is.

In the dark of night, his bed seemed terribly empty. His house was empty. His life was empty. He thanked God that Eliza was there to help hold things together.

Francis was bolstered by Eliza and was cheered by the two grandchildren. But Francis would be tested again, and he would lose still more of what is important in his life.

# CHAPTER 11

# *Invasion*

In early June 1864, villagers heard that Federal forces were in Lexington and were headed toward Bedford County and Lynchburg. Father and daughter speculated about what might happen, or could happen, or what would happen to them.

Bedford families hid their valuables. Eliza stashed the Cornish silverware in the barn, deep under the hay. Another family was said to have dropped their silverware in a well. Francis buried one of his shotguns in the hay and slid the other under a pile of clothes in his room.

In the village, the postmaster-telegrapher, Noel Butler, hid his key and the crank dynamo.

Francis said, "Maybe the Federals will soon get to Richmond, too. Then the war will be over. That would be good. I don't see how this war is worth it. End it all. Stop the killing."

Eliza spoke from her heart, "Maybe. And then Byron and Caleb can come home."

In mid-June, the Union Army of General David Hunter trudged toward them from the east, from Lynchburg and the Town of Liberty, pressing toward Western Virginia, Hunter's homeland.

This was the army of 15,000 which had come from Lexington, where the Federals burned the VMI library, hospital, barracks, and other buildings. They skirmished on the outskirts of Lynchburg. Hunter commandeered Sandusky, the home of George Hutter, outside of the city, and during the night General Jubal Early's forces, assisted by some Virginia Military Institute cadets and cheering citizens, maneuvered to mislead Hunter into believing that the defenders had superior force and that an attack would fail.

Hunter's men were low on ammunition. They were hungry and tired. Hunter decided not to attempt to seize the city. Humiliated by failing to capture Lynchburg, he vacated Sandusky and headed west, back through the Bedford County county seat, the Town of Liberty.

Some of General McCausland's cavalry chased them. Bedford county snipers and bushwhackers in the hills came down to harass and raid them as they hustled toward Buford's Gap.

Hunter's men had been living off the land wherever they had gone. Painfully low on provisions, they seized whatever food and supplies they could find. Though the Cornish farm was several miles north of the primary east-west route, it was vulnerable to Hunter's marauding soldiers combing the countryside.

It was dusk, June 20th, when the enemy neared. The Cornishes heard sporadic distant gunfire and occasional yelling. The family clustered together just outside the door to the house. An officer on horseback finally appeared, with rifle at the ready. Six raggedy soldiers, carrying partly filled bags, plodded behind.

Francis and Henry knew they were outnumbered and outgunned. They stood in front of Eliza and the children, trying to appear confident and unafraid and not belligerent or hostile. Ezekiel and Adam stood between the family and the barn.

One of these men might have been the very man who killed Newton. Just the thought made Francis grit his teeth. For Eliza and the children, he contained his anger as the intruders entered his yard.

Looking at the man on the horse, he asked, "Where have you been?"

"Virginia, mostly"

"What do you want?"

"Food. That's all. Now. Quick!"

"Help yourself."

Francis saw them as dangerous, this bunch of tired, unhealthy young men. One was barefoot. Francis surprised himself when he became aware of feeling some sympathy for them.

The leader gestured toward the house, pointed to the corral and barn. The men knew what to do: they had done it often before.

Two headed for the big gray barn—it seemed taller than the house—with a coop attached and the nearby corral. They chased—and caught—about a half dozen chickens, snapping their necks and throwing the limp birds into their bags. One grabbed a small pig and stuffed it, still squealing, in a bag. They glanced at the huge hog and then at their leader. He shook his head; apparently it was too big a project and they didn't have the hours needed to slaughter the big beast. Their loss: that animal was a lot of ham, pork and bacon.

The Federals eyed the sturdy old farm wagon, but saw its broken wheel. They don't have time to fix it. They left it be. The family buggy seemed too fragile and frail.

To the two men who had stomped into the house, the leader called, "Bring out the good stuff."

Out they came. One had his mouth stuffed with bread and was carrying a pail of water and a big bread loaf under one arm and a bag of salt under the other. He put them down near the leader and darted back in. He soon reemerged while digging honey from a big jar, using his fingers as a spoon, barely holding a bag of hominy next to his chest. The other fellow hugged a slab of bacon and chunks of smoked venison while carrying a bag of flour.

"Get those horses. Only the good ones."

They found halters and led away the two best horses, Atlas and Hercules, those strong enough to carry riders, leaving only two young scrawny ones. One soldier jumped bareback onto Atlas. Bags were tied and thrown over Hercules.

"Come on. Come on. Go. Get going! It's getting dark. We don't want to be left behind here!"

Adam and Ezekiel didn't say a word. They looked at each other and nodded. Both must have been thinking, "Here, now, the North is here. This is what we have waited for. This is the moment. Freedom is now."

As the raiders walked away, the slave brothers did, too, with nothing more than the clothes they were wearing. Free at last. Together they jogged west with Hunter's swarm.

The Federals and some 265 escaping Bedford county slaves tramped away. Soon the last of the Federal stragglers left Buford's, and the sounds of the marching, marauding army faded.

Then they were really gone. And it began to rain.

The Cornishes took stock. The greatest loss: Ezekiel and Adam.

They were grateful that the invaders didn't hurt the family or torch the house or the barn. They lost valuable food. They lost two fine horses. They still had two young horses, Dolly and Samson.

"At least they didn't get the silverware or the gun we hid in the barn," said Eliza. Henry added, "Or my stash up in my apple tree!"

"I guess they didn't see the cows or the sheep."

The hurried raiders had not scoured the area very thoroughly. They didn't discover the animals that Francis and Eliza had scattered up into the wooded hills just before the Federal forces came.

Francis retrieved his two cows and his six sheep while worrying who would do the work of the farm.

The slave brothers had been precious property—the manpower engines of the farm. "All of us will have to work harder than ever before. You too, Henry. Thank God that Eliza is here. The only other sure thing is the bees: they will work as always. They will make us some honey."

Still around, somewhere, was the peculiar Mr. Hallock. He would have had very little of what the Federals needed.

Henry opined, "They probably got nothing at all from Mr. Hallock."

Eliza had first noticed this ominous fellow shortly after he arrived in Buford's in 1863 and moved in to an austere cabin on an adjacent tract.

A burly man, Clinton Hallock was bigger than any of the Cornish men—six feet tall, unkempt long hair, a full gray, tobacco-stained beard, a bit overweight, weathered face, and dark, deep-set eyes. He said he was a native of Staunton and that he was wounded "in the belly" during a battle on a scouting mission "in the Valley" and was "sent home" because he had become unable to use a rifle. With "family money" he bought an old slave cabin and fifteen acres of stony hillside from the estate of Tinsley Molson, saying then he wanted a new start after his wife had deserted him. There were rumors that she had just disappeared one night without saying goodbye to anyone, not even her best friends. Another story was that he was a deserter. Still another rumor was that the Army threw him out because he shot a fellow soldier.

He raised a few vegetables. He had no animals, no horse, not even a dog. He did trap for meat. He was a loner, without friends. He wasn't one to converse very much. No relatives came to see him. Townsfolk kept their distance.

Hallock devoted much of his time to just watching people. Eliza was his favorite.

On one occasion, as she was preparing supper, one of the dogs began growling. She thought she heard someone outside the window. And another night, after she had tucked in her children, one dog growled a bit, and then was silent. She decided she had been imagining that someone had been watching.

But the next day, her father found that one of the dogs had died during the night. He guessed "he must have eaten a sick rabbit or something."

When Eliza took the buggy to the village, Hallock often conjured an excuse to walk to town, too. The heart of the Buford's community was the country store, run by Noel Butler, who was also the depot telegraph operator and postmaster. Hallock would loom in to the store. She was uncomfortable about his interest in her and her family. He often asked the same question: "Where is your husband?"

One time, he sidled next to her when she was talking intently with the telegrapher. He just stood there, menacingly. She concluded her conversation in a whisper. She turned away when Hallock asked, "When is your husband coming home?" She raised her head high, ignored him and briskly walked out.

His question made her angry—angry that he was so nosy, and angry that she desperately didn't know the answer herself. She wished Byron were home right then. He would make the strange man leave her alone. How she missed Byron!

On rare occasions the telegraph operator had brief messages for Eliza from her husband in Richmond. One afternoon, as she began to organize supper, she had a premonition that she would be seeing Byron soon, sooner than anyone would suspect. She was right.

That very afternoon, Noel Butler rode out to the farm with this message:

TO FRANCIS CORNISH AT BUFORDS.
TRAIN BRINGING REMAINS OF NEWTON
& COUSIN ALBERT. HAVE WAGON READY.
CALEB.

Eliza asked her father, "What day? And who is Cousin Albert?"

"I don't know. We'll just go every day."

"Maybe Byron is coming, too! I hope it's tonight!" exclaimed Eliza, "I'll stay with the children."

Francis said he would go to meet the Lynchburg train, which usually came after sundown, and wait. He would go tonight, tomorrow and the next day, if need be.

# CHAPTER 12

# *Depot*

At sundown, Francis is waiting at the depot, with his old wagon drawn by the young, but obedient, horses, Dolly and Samson. Hours pass. The sun sets. Francis tells himself to wait a few more hours. He dozes.

The train is always an event, day or night. The sound of its coming attracts curious residents.

It is near midnight when the train from Lynchburg slows to Buford's depot, where it will take on water. Conductor Lancaster is accustomed to stopping his train here. The trackside tank is always full of water which is fed by springs from above the Tiber.

By the time the train actually stops, Francis is awake and alert. Byron and Caleb are ready to unload their precious cargo and escort it to the Cornish farm. They smile upon seeing Francis Cornish standing by his wagon at the tie post. Four curious bystanders, including Clinton Hallock, watch.

The box car door is open. Out jump Caleb and Byron. "Hello Father!" Caleb shakes his father's hand as Byron salutes and says, "Hello Francis. Good to see you." Then, "Quick, before the train twitches, help us unload the coffins."

Francis compresses Byron's hands and says, "Good to see you! Good to see you, Son! Thank God you have Newton! And your cousin Albert."

Francis comes to the car and helps the two officers unload the heavy coffins.

The bystanders stare as the ominous boxes are put on the wagon. The observers even bow their heads. Too many young officers had come home that way. Byron speaks loud enough so Hallock can hear, "The boys will be buried tomorrow." In less than two minutes the coffins are on the wagon.

Conductor Lancaster looks back at the moonlit men with the coffins. He thinks to himself, They have to go to Ironville. More often than not, there are no wagons at the depot. He wonders, It's almost as though they were expected. That's strange. Just lucky, I guess.

The engineer concentrates on his dials and knobs and the train starts forward. The officers salute as the train pulls out, but there is no one looking back to respond.

A few minutes later, as his train runs at night speed past Ironville, Conductor Lancaster again wonders, "How come there were people waiting at Buford's?" Then he has an idea, "Well, I guess when something involves the President's family, they get messages to where they want. Good. It will be almost dawn when I get to Salem."


Meanwhile, Byron and Francis settle onto the front seat and Francis drives away from the depot. Caleb yawns, leans his back against a coffin and hooks his right arm over the side of the wagon, legs dangling out the back. He savors the wonderfully familiar sights, illuminated by moonlight, for a few moments until shut out by eyes heavy with fatigue.

"Byron, where did they find Newton?" asks Francis.

"It's a long story, a very sad story, Francis. I'll give you the details in a minute. First, tell me, how are my dear wife and children?"

"They're home. The children are fine. Eliza is fine. They want to see you. We heard that the Federals had captured Richmond. I am so glad you got away, and you look good."

Francis somberly concentrates on the meandering road which roughly parallels the creek, slowly rising towards the mountains miles away. Somewhere behind, Hallock is walking, but farther and farther behind them until he finally turns off the road towards his cabin.

Francis again presses his question. "Where did you find Newton? What really happened to him?"

Byron looks around left and right. Then he takes a deep breath, "I'm sorry. I misled you. We still don't know where Newton is. He is not here, he is not on the wagon. He is not in one of the coffins."

Francis gasps. A minute passes as the sad reality soaks in. Finally, he asks, "Well, who is in the coffins?"

Byron answers, "Nobody at all." Francis looks incredulous. Byron adds, "I'll explain."

He describes the plan about the Treasury reserve and the imaginary Cousin Albert. His father-in-law nods, first slowly, and then vigorously. The men sit more erect. About a dozen minutes away from the depot, they turn off the road and follow the trail across a meadow and up to the log farmhouse where Eliza is waiting.

Eliza dashes out to greet them, "Oh Byron, Byron! How wonderful you are home! Good! Good!"

She twists around and exclaims, "Caleb, my big brother, Caleb! So wonderful to see you! And you look good, too!"

Byron slides off the wagon and fervently hugs and kisses his wife. The children, she explains, are sound asleep. Eliza listens attentively as Byron explains what they must do next. "Where is Henry?"

"Up at his place," replies Eliza.

"Good. Leave him there. We don't want him to know anything about what we are doing. If he comes down, keep him away from the barn. But get him down to the cemetery for the funeral in the morning. Right now, Caleb and I have work to do."

Eliza says, "Byron, hurry. Get it done. Hurry. I've been waiting so long to see you."

"I'll tell you all about it—even about cousin Albert. Wait for me."

She and her father walk back into the house.

The men remount the wagon and head past Ezekiel's vacant cabin and down a slight grade below and behind the house. Caleb hops off and opens the corral gate. At the barn, he undoes the harness and reins, smacks Dolly and Samson on their rumps and chases them into the corral. He and Byron push the wagon inside the barn. Byron looks around and sees no one, not even Hallock, whose view is obscured by the hill.

Caleb finds the lantern in its regular place, lights it, and pulls the door shut. Byron grabs one shovel and hands another to Caleb. Both men start digging into the dirt floor. Though tired, they dig with vigor, knowing that here, their mission is almost complete. They create a hole big enough to bury a cow.

Caleb climbs into the wagon. He removes the coffin lids and hands bag after bag down to Byron, who packs them carefully into the hole. Caleb then shovels the excess dirt up into the coffins and nails the lids back on. He brushes any tell tale soil out of the wagon bed. The loaded coffins are ready for burial tomorrow.

Now dirt covers the bags, the barn floor is smoothed and covered with loose hay pulled down from the loft. As if of one mind, they step directly over the buried gold and jewelry. Byron says, "Well done, Lieutenant Cornish!" Caleb smiles, "Thank you, Captain. My compliments to you, too, sir...Byron." They shake hands and grab each other's shoulders—and both give deep sighs. They stare at the floor for a few moments, as if to be certain that the reserve is really there. Byron douses the lantern. Caleb very measuredly closes the door as they leave.

In the Cornish barn, this reserve of the Confederate Treasury will be safe from the Yankees!

Back at the house, Martha and Daniel are asleep in the "girls room" that Eliza has been sharing with them. Byron tiptoes into the dim room and kneels beside the bed. He studies them for a minute or two and then kisses each forehead. They don't even stir. He tiptoes out. Francis has retired to his room and is asleep. Caleb plops down on the floor in the big room, curls up near the fire, and falls asleep before Byron can even wish him "good dreams."

Byron hears Eliza moving around up in the loft where "the boys" had slept while growing up. He ascends the steep wooden stairs, drawn by gentle lantern light coming from the loft doorway. He will be alone with Eliza at last.

She lays her hairbrush on the small table next to the door. Her hair softly curls about her shoulders. The white muslin nightgown is unbuttoned, revealing soft, smooth skin. A soldier's dream. She reaches out to him, hungrily staring into his eyes. He extinguishes the lantern.

Later, Byron sleeps especially well.


Early the next morning, Henry, Caleb, Byron and Francis dig pits for the two coffins in the family cemetery on the wooded knoll. A few paces from the grave marker stones of Eliza's mother and grandparents, an unpretentious but solemn ceremony will be held. About midmorning, Caleb and Byron drive the wagon from the barnyard to the cemetery. The men remove the coffins and carefully lay them to rest. Henry, unaware of what is really going on, solemnly does his share.

Then, not wanting to appear ignorant, he mumbles, "I didn't know Albert. A relative of Byron?"

Eliza sees Hallock watching from afar and wonders if he suspects anything. She advises her father to "Make it look good." Heads bow as Francis speaks what sounds like the right words and picks up soil and sprinkles it over the graves of the "dead soldiers." Henry covers the boxes. Caleb takes his pistol and fires it into the air. Byron takes out his pistol a moment later and shoots it into the air. Eliza begins singing "Amazing Grace" and the men join in.

They walk slowly, with heads down, back to the house.

Inside, Francis Cornish reluctantly admits that the digging and lifting has been too much: he strained his back. He would have to neglect some of his usual work for a few days. Eliza was already overloaded with chores. Henry offers to help tomorrow when he can and then goes home.

Byron decides to stay to help out for a day or so, until his father-in-law feels a bit better. He also wants to listen around to make sure no one—especially Hallock—suspects what they had done. He pulls rank on Caleb and orders him to head south to join up with the Presidential party and report to Davis and Trenholm that the mission was a success.

On the morning of April 6, Caleb saddles up Dolly, bids his farm home farewell, and heads south toward Danville.


Three days later, Byron is still at the farm when villagers were passing the word that General Robert E. Lee surrendered at Appomattox. A cloud of confusion settles over them all.

Is the Confederacy finished? Should Byron try to rejoin Davis? Or should he stay close to the treasure to guard it? Where is Caleb? Ambrose? David?

# CHAPTER 13

## *Defeat*

Events of 1865 shake both the North and the South. Lee surrenders at Appomattox. President Lincoln is assassinated on April 14. Jefferson Davis and his family flee southward. Colonel Ambrose Bothwell holds at Danville, but surrenders there on the 27th. General Johnston, farther south with remnant CSA forces, gives up on the 29th.

Jefferson Davis makes it to Georgia, but is captured on May 10th. The Confederate treasury is nowhere to be found. Davis claims that the Treasury assets which departed with him from Richmond were disbursed to needy CSA troops along the way. Not everyone believes him. There are rumors that some were dropped off in North Carolina and buried.

Much of Richmond lies in ruin. Officially, the States are a nation reunited, but the union is tenuous and unstable. The Federal government rescinds Virginia's sovereignty and appoints Francis Pierpont as governor, ruling the state from an office in Alexandria. Southern states are distrusted and under military scrutiny. Lincoln's successor, Andrew Johnson, is nobody's hero.

Confederate soldiers are allowed to go home. Many top officials are held. The war has taken a terrible toll of lost or broken lives—on both sides. Thousands have died. Thousands are wounded or disabled. Byron, Caleb and David are lucky ones: they were alive and with bodies intact. Ambrose has a troublesome wrist. They are weary, but healthy and relieved to be home.

The Cornish tobacco field had been neglected. Small saplings and cedars had sprung up. Caleb is ready to help his father run Valley Meadow Farm. Within a week of arriving home, he proposes to Mary Hannah Caldwell, a Buford girl he had known since childhood. She had been hoping that he would.

Caleb and his father and Uncle Henry will concentrate on nurturing some vegetables to preserve and tending the sheep and swine. Until they can get help, field crops must be postponed.

Byron and brother David will help revitalize their father's business. Byron, Eliza and the children are back in their home in Lynchburg. He tells Eliza, "It's so good to be back in our own home. I missed you and the children. We don't have to hide from the Yankees anymore. We don't have to make up stories. No more lies. No more deception." They hug.

Ambrose is pleasantly surprised by the greeting he receives upon returning home to Lynchburg from Danville. Henrietta hugs him with an embrace more passionate than he could remember. This tall, slim woman, with brown hair tightly coiled atop her head, is usually reserved, controlled, almost prudishly proper. She is the Presbyterian preacher's daughter who only socializes at church events. She enjoys reading at home. She always had admired her husband, yet never seemed to be able to admit strong feelings for him. After five years of cool marriage, she is still childless and feeling unfulfilled. While he was away, she realized how much she needed him. This reunion seems to be about catching up and starting a new beginning.

Hundreds of Confederate leaders are charged with high treason; many are imprisoned. Some of the victors plan to put Robert E. Lee on trial. Trenholm spends only two months in a Tennessee jail; his prior business relationships with northern enterprises works to his advantage. Even a few Union generals recommend that he be pardoned. He is freed in the autumn.

Virginians try to celebrate Christmas, relieved that the war is over, but burdened with sadness for lost family, friends, and way of life.


The Treasury men feel as many defeated soldiers do: proud of having completed a difficult mission, but unable to get recognition for a job well done.

As months go by, they wrestle with a dilemma. What should they do with the buried Treasury? Give it to the reunited nation ruled by Yankees? Give it to the state of Virginia ruled by Yankees?

They believe that it belongs to the South and agree that since it was Trenholm who had assigned them to their secret mission, they might look to him for guidance as to what to do now. Colonel Ambrose Bothwell will travel to see him at Charleston in January.

Ambrose is impressed how Trenholm has been able to repossess his elegant home, now almost empty. Yankees carried off most furnishings and paintings. All silverware and most glassware is gone. His former house slaves have gone. He has persuaded some other freed slaves to help run his house in exchange for room and board. Daughter Mary Jo has been managing housekeeping details, but she will leave in June when she marries a long-time Charleston friend and war veteran. Ambrose tells himself that he will have to tell David to erase her from his list of marital prospects.

What to do with the reserve? Trenholm's first comment is that he has no personal interest in any of the money. "I don't want any of it. To start with, it is not mine. If I take any of that money, it would go against my very nature: it would be too easy."

Ambrose is skeptical. He has worked with this man and knows that he is an enterprising businessman at heart—an entrepreneur who thrives on dealing and making money. He wonders, "Here the team has access to significant assets, yet he doesn't want any of it."

Ambrose cannot hide his doubts: he frowns. Trenholm decides to continue, "I like doing things that others would think are impossible. I am going to forge ahead on my own. I built my business before from scratch, and I can do it again. I will line up some partners, might even get some Yankees, and with them start generating profits, without even needing a dime of my own money! I enjoy having tough goals. I don't like it if it is too easy." He smiles. "The South will rise again."

He advises Ambrose, "Colonel, you and your fellows—sit tight. Just let it rest for a while until we see how this all unfolds. As you can see, I will be all right here. But you men can take some of it for your immediate needs. Consider it to be overdue compensation for extraordinary service."

And they did.

The Cornish barn is now a bank, a very exclusive bank, with only a handful of customers. No marble floors. No fancy facade. Though just a gray barn, it is a special bank, a secret subterranean vault.

For the first withdrawal, Caleb chases the chickens out, shuts the barn door and gets to work with a shovel. He digs a bit, reaches down into a bag and retrieves rolls of gold eagle coins. Again and again he pulls out a roll, until he has four, with twenty coins each for Ambrose, Byron, David, and himself. He closes the bag, shovels dirt into the hole, and spreads hay to cover his traces.

He opens the door to leave and finds two inquisitive chickens looking in. It means nothing to them that the vast bulk of the transferred Confederate Treasury assets are left there in the ground. Nothing valuable there but old hay seeds. Better pickings outside. They cluck away.

Robert E. Lee had been right that "Lynchburg or some place west (would be) the most advantageous place to which to remove stores from Richmond." Lynchburg was indeed spared, physically. Its buldings and bridges escaped the ruination and destruction suffered by many Southern cities. But the city and neighboring Bedford County lost many hundreds of men killed in action or dead from infected wounds or disease.

Before the war, Lynchburg had been a vital hub of southern commerce, a more important center of tobacco trade than even Richmond. Could Lynchburg regain the prosperity it once knew? In 1866 there are glimmers of progress.

Ambrose Bothwell and Byron Rugerman are involved in their father's businesses.

The Bothwells are surviving this "Federalized Virginia" period better than most families. Attorney James Bothwell is an experienced politician who weaves new networks from well-established personal connecting threads.

Father James welcomes Ambrose into his law practice. Ambrose can help manage the affairs of estates, survivors, and untangle contracts contorted by broken relationships and failed businesses. Ambrose and Henrietta had indeed celebrated the end of four years of war; twin girls are born in the spring of 1866.

Byron and David join their father's brokerage business which is struggling to regain some degree of the good fortune it once enjoyed. Demand for tobacco is unabated, but supply of Virginia-grown tobacco is down more than 50 percent. Lack of adequate labor—with most slaves gone from the farms— means less planting, less cultivation, and less harvesting.

Charles Rugerman asks his sons to travel and find new tobacco suppliers, perhaps Kentucky or farther west, and possibly entirely new lines of business.

The young men convince more nearby farmers that the Rugerman firm is the best wholesaler around. Byron tells them, "You do what you do best: farm. We will do what we do best: deal." He likes brokering, whether it be tobacco, farm produce, or whatever.

Byron is confident that old classmates and friends from Virginia Military Institute will open some doors for him. David will initiate his own contacts, traveling to explore new markets in the North.

# CHAPTER 14

## *Renewal*

This is a quiet time for the bags of gold and jewelry resting comfortably down in the dirt floor of the Cornish barn. Now and then Caleb pulls the carriage out or swaps tools. Many days go by when the only action is a mouse scurrying across the floor. Elsewhere in America and in Virginia, times are changing.

The House of Representatives impeaches President Johnson, but the Senate acquits him in 1868. There is a money panic in 1869 and a shortage of ready gold.

Virginia emerges from under Federal management and resumes being governed by the people of Virginia in January 1870.

Will the Confederacy rise again? Will patriots of Virginia need the hidden assets to fight again?

Hopes fade when beloved Robert E. Lee dies in the fall of 1870. Even the optimists acknowledge that the war really is over. Most Southerners, and especially Virginians, grieve the loss of their respected and honorable leader.

Back at Buford's, Francis Cornish's brother Henry is ailing. He has been coughing more and more. In recent months he has lost weight and now has a distinctly gray look. The local doctor tells him it is consumption. He knows his time on earth is nearing the end.

Just before Henry, a bachelor all his life, lapses, he quietly tells his brother, "You're a good brother, Francis. You have been good to me. You have a fine family. I want them to have whatever is mine. It's in my will. All is to go to Caleb, Eliza and their children."

Francis tries to comfort him, "You've been a wonderful brother, too, Henry. God will welcome you to Heaven." He pats his brother on the shoulder—and the dying man raises his hand.

"And you know what…I did bring home gold from California. It is in the old apple tree by my house."

Francis is unsure if this is just the delirious fantasy of a dying man. He says, "Yes, Henry. Yes, you did." Henry nods feebly and gently passes away.

Francis finds the handwritten will. It makes no mention of any gold. It does make clear that Henry's 120-acre farm is to go to his niece and nephew, Eliza Rugerman and Caleb Cornish, and their families. Henry shunned niece Katherine and her Yankee husband.

The following day, the Cornish family gathers at its hillside cemetery. For a change, Henry doesn't have to dig a hole or carry a coffin or shovel dirt atop a coffin. He has a free ride. Caleb and Francis dig the hole and fill in the dirt over the coffin.

In the main house, the family reminisces about Henry and what he meant to them. Francis tells the others about Henry's dying words. They read the will.

After lunch, Eliza says to her brother, "Now that Henry's place is ours—it's been quite a while since I've been in it—let's go see what's there." Then, with a twinkle in her eye, she adds, "And while we're at it, let's inspect his apple tree."

Eliza carries a chair from Henry's porch and sets it beside the tree. Caleb steps up on the seat and stretches to reach a hollow in the fork of the trunk. Mindful of possible wasps, Caleb gingerly explores the hole.

Suddenly, "I found something! A leather pouch." He holds it up, a small bag, about the size of an apple. "Here," he tosses it. Eliza catches it and is surprised. It weighs almost as much as a small watermelon.

In Henry's house, they empty the bag onto the table and out fall a few gold coins and an assortment of nuggets. Caleb estimates that Henry's stash is worth at least $1,000 and maybe almost $2,000. Eliza says, "The rumor was true all along. Thank you, Uncle Henry!"


Caleb and his father are eking out a living on the farm, now restored to its original 360 acres. They manage to attract a former slave family to help work the farm in exchange for living in Henry's house. It is agreed that, as tenant farmers, they will derive a quarter of the farm's yield and also be free to use ten acres for their own family gardens and crops. Eliza comes from Lynchburg to help from time to time.

Clinton Hallock has not moved. He still watches almost everyone. Once, at the village store, Hallock asked Caleb, "Why do you work in your barn and keep your barn shut on hot days?" Caleb looked up at him and just shrugged his shoulders to say it isn't important.


In Lynchburg, these are hopeful years. New businesses spring up. Ambrose and Byron set up new enterprises, separate from their fathers, but with seed money from the fathers.

James Bothwell threaded his way through government hurdles, cashed in old political favors, and won a state charter for his son to start a bank. Ambrose runs it as chairman; wife Henrietta blazes a trail for women by serving as secretary-treasurer. Other board members are Byron, Caleb and David. They agree that the name seems appropriate and impressive:

Mountain City Deposit Trust Company. The actual managing executive committee is composed of Ambrose, Byron and Henrietta. Ambrose leases some ground floor space in a solid-looking stone building on Main Street. They start wooing depositors.

The elder Rugerman set aside some space at his offices to help his sons Byron and David; he helped win an agent agreement with a Baltimore insurance underwriter. Thus begins a new insurance and brokerage business, which they name the Universal Guaranty and Assurance Company. Its offices are on the second floor of a brick building a few doors away from Bothwell's Trust Company. Byron heads the enterprise, aided by David as New Accounts Manager. Ambrose and Caleb will be on the board, and the Rugermans also break tradition: they invite Eliza to be on the board.

Both families help each other and refer clients to each other. Caleb, over in Bedford County, works the farm. David is often traveling. As a practical matter, both the Trust Company and the Assurance Company are run by Ambrose Bothwell and Byron Rugerman.


Caleb wants to acquire more livestock. Byron's and Ambrose's businesses need significantly more working capital to expand facilities and services. Like a slick book jacket, the impressive name of each company belies the minimal capital inside.

They debate what to do about the buried treasure in the barn. They rationalize a second withdrawal for overdue compensation. Some of the reserve assets would be a great help in financing their enterprises. But before they help themselves, they decide to see the old boss for guidance. Again, it seems like an appropriate time to confer with Trenholm.

This time, it is Byron Rugerman who makes the trip to Charleston.

He finds his old boss as dynamic as ever—even enthusiastic. George Trenholm emerged from bankruptcy in 1867 and is climbing a new upward spiral of success. More than four years have passed since the war ended. Like thousands of other businessmen, farmers and merchants, Trenholm strives to recapture the thriving prosperity of prewar days. He works almost around the clock. He refreshed his links to London, New York, and Philadelphia from his base in Charleston. Former creditors backed him because of his reputation and talent for success.

Trenholm again reminds Rugerman that the reserve is not the team's money and never has been. He counsels, "You could extract still more from the hoard. But this time, you will owe back. Whatever you withdraw, understand that you are trustees, trustees for the people. Use the money to help those who will do good for the South."

Byron reports back to Ambrose, Caleb and David. They opt to withdraw $500 each now, not as back pay, but as loans, and feel authorized to do more later.

Caleb again volunteers to make the actual "bank withdrawal." He completes his daily farm chores late one afternoon, brings a strong shoe box from the house, and then, with the door shut, free from any prying eyes, he digs into the Confederate lode.

He reaches into the bag he had tapped before but decides to let that one be and instead access a different bag, to see that deeper bags aren't rotting in the ground. He probes cautiously and finds the top of another bag. From inside he scoops up a roll of coins and—to his surprise—a pair of jeweled earrings hooked to each other.

He pauses, wondering how he might divide one pair of earrings among four ex-treasury men. Devoid of an idea, Caleb sets the earrings aside for the moment and fishes out rolls of gold eagles totaling 200 coins, almost eight pounds, for distribution.

He is putting the coins in the shoe box when he hears footsteps approaching the barn. He frantically pushes dirt back into the hole and pulls handfuls of hay over the box and the loose dirt. He springs to the door and hears a rattling of the latch.

He yanks open the door and finds big Clinton Hallock. Caleb steps out and closes the door behind himself. "Hello. What do you want?"

"Why do have the door shut when you are inside on such a hot day?"

Caleb instinctively obliges to answer a question, "We don't want the chickens in." But sensing more than mere idle curiosity on Hallock's part, he demands, "What business have you here?"

"Just wondering."

Caleb straightens and steps closer to his larger, unwanted visitor, "Well, why don't you just 'wonder' on home." And with that, almost nose to nose, without touching him, crowds him and crowds him until Hallock turns away and heads home. Caleb follows until he is certain the man is far gone and out of sight.

Caleb reenters the barn and properly refills the hole and disguises his work. The earrings have gone out of sight and out of his mind.

Back in his kitchen, while Hannah is in the village, Caleb makes four piles each with two rolls and ten loose eagles, worth $500 per pile, on the table. He wraps each carefully in paper. He puts his above a kitchen beam, out of sight. The other three packages go into the shoe box. He will take them to Lynchburg in his pockets on his next opportunity.


Ambrose, Byron and David each use their coins to help feed their ventures.

Byron's $500 helps his enterprise move ahead. If asked who is behind the business, Byron alludes to a generous father and to "private investors from New England." Ambrose explains his support comes from his family, pooling of estate accounts, and an "anonymous philanthropist." Shading the truth comes easily now.

Caleb buys more sheep and plans to enlarge the family home place. If anyone questions where he got the money, he says, "I'm grateful for Uncle Henry and other relatives." If a villager brings up the rumor that Henry had thousands and thousands of dollars hidden in a tree, Caleb has a practiced answer: "Think what you want to think, but my daddy always taught me that money doesn't grow on trees."

Most of the assets still lay underground.

Life is improving for the Bothwells, the Rugermans and the Cornishes. They take satisfaction from their success in their enterprises. They also share deeper pride, almost smugness, for having completed a complex mission for the Confederacy.

But they begin to think beyond their own businesses. They reflect what the former Treasury Secretary was urging: use the assets for the benefit of as many people as possible. Nurture new businesses or support community services. The idea rattles around in the back of their minds. If they concentrate on it, they will find a way.

From time to time, Caleb and Eliza would think back to Uncle Henry with gratitude for his generosity to them. His passing was sad, but they were not badly troubled by Henry's death. They assured themselves it was the right time. He was spared further pain and discomfort. Their contentment is more seriously shaken in 1875.

Francis Cornish suffers a massive heart attack, right in the middle of summer harvest, and dies two days later. He was 67. The Cornishes, the Rugermans and the tenant farmers all mourn. He was a good man, an honest man. His six Virginia grandchildren, ranging in age from 4 to 17, know they have lost an important pillar of their lives, but cannot comprehend the respect their parents feel for Francis Cornish III.

After the funeral, the Treasury team strolls back to the house. Caleb pauses and leans on the gate to the barnyard. Eliza joins him, and he puts his arm around her shoulders. Byron, David, and Ambrose soberly view the scenery.

Caleb and Eliza feel a deep loss. Francis was their father who sired them, who raised them, who taught them, who provided for them, who loved them. They feel a big hole in their hearts. Finally, Ambrose breaks the silence and calmly reminds them that "no one lives forever."

Byron protests, "He was only 67. That is not really that much older than we are. I'm beginning to realize how mortal I am. Eliza lost brother Newton. The rest of us escaped death and serious injury in the war. The Good Lord spared us. Why? Are we alive and well to serve some special purpose?"

Ambrose slowly responds, "Byron, I feel the same way. I came out of it with just a hurt wrist. Compared with so many who lost more, I am truly blessed. We're so much better off than most other people. You know, we'd talked a while ago about helping people and our community. That barn bank has helped our ventures to succeed. When we repay what we borrowed, that bank could help others as it helped us. Well, I've been thinking how we can do that."

"How?" asks Caleb.

Ambrose outlines the idea of a rotating loan fund. He obviously has been mulling the idea over. They would start by borrowing from the barn bank. The Fund would lend money, at low interest for up to five years, to constructive community ventures and promising projects that would broaden economic prosperity. As loans were repaid, the money would be recycled to finance other useful enterprises. This would be a low-profile

94

rehabilitation plan which would also make outright grants for special community needs.

Eliza suggests, "It could be called The Community Fund."

Ambrose nods his approval and continues to explain the idea.

The fund could work out of the bank's offices, with a guiding board made up of Ambrose, Byron, and their wives. As the fund progressed, it would openly accept contributions from philanthropists to build the fund. By drawing from the barn bank from time to time, they could inject more capital into the fund, and, if questions arose, they would allude to donors who wish to remain anonymous.

The Community Fund takes root in their minds. Soon they will make it real.

The United States celebrates its centennial with a big exposition in Philadelphia. But the year ends on a somber note.

In December, in his Charleston office, George Trenholm collapses and dies. His doctor says it was a massive heart attack. Byron and Ambrose feel that they have lost not only a good boss, but a good friend, a big brother, an inspiration. They know that the south has lost an important citizen.

Trenholm is gone. The Confederacy is long gone. Only a dreamer would think that the South will rise again. To whom should they be loyal? Who shall set policy now?

Ambrose feels a new responsibility. With his Confederate Treasury mentor dead, Ambrose assumes that as the senior member of the team the burden of decision and policy is now upon him. Never lacking confidence, he considers this a natural mandate and believes that he will be the ultimate authority on how the buried assets should be used.

Shortly thereafter, he decides to start the loan program immediately. He is approached at his bank by a distinguished looking gentleman with a military air who said he was from Atlanta and was looking to start a new cigar factory to be his new Virginia division. He wanted a $200 loan for just a week to secure the rent on a building (unrevealed as to where, due to negotiations). His name was Weyman Alderson, and he supported his request with sketches of his proposed operation, a simplified sales forecast, and even samples of his cigar labels. He spoke of noted politicians in Washington who would vouch for his credibility. Ambrose was impressed by Alderson's apparent competence and breeding. He believed the venture would be good for Lynchburg.

At a morning meeting, without consulting either Byron or Caleb, Ambrose has Alderson sign a loan agreement and then hands him a roll of twenty gold eagles. The businessman invites Ambrose to be his guest for lunch at the Hotel Lynch, where he is staying, at which time he can meet the shop manager, Harold Eastland.

Upon arriving at the dining room, Ambrose finds that his host is not there. Neither is manager Eastland. Ambrose waits and waits. Finally, he goes to the desk to inquire about Alderson's whereabouts only to learn that the hotel had never seen either of the two men from Atlanta.

After two weeks, Ambrose concludes that he will never see Alderson—or the $200—again.

With new humility, Ambrose tells the others about his overzealousness and his error of judgment in failing to check facts that could be checked. "I'm not as sure of myself as I was. It appears that I'm not as good a judge of character as I thought. We'll confer together from now on. Maybe work out some kind of screening process."

They agree that they must resist the urge to hurry to dig up all the reserve. They need to take the time to prepare this loan program well. Prudence got them this far. Prudence must prevail.

# CHAPTER 15

## *Story*

Now who knows about the hoard? There are just five people who know everything: Ambrose, Byron, Caleb, David, and Eliza.

How much has Ambrose told Henrietta? How much has she deduced?

If and when they do recover all the assets, how will they explain their sudden wealth? If they reveal the assets, they need to consider the consequences; their reputations for integrity could be jeopardized.

Byron comes up with an idea to create a cover story to "launder" the gold and jewelry: publicize a secret treasure. Then, after some time, if they need to explain their new wealth, they can say they had found the secret treasure.

Ambrose finally tells Henrietta everything. She had sensed something anyway. The two explore what they might do. She suggests that the treasure story be printed and they might even make some money by then selling copies to the public. Of course, the story should not reveal where the hoard really is.

Byron, Ambrose and Henrietta conceive a tale about a group of Virginia adventurers who discover gold and silver out West back in 1820 or so. These men find so much of the precious metals that they need several trips to bring it all home. On the second trip, they swap much of the silver for jewelry in St. Louis to reduce the weight of their loads. While back in Virginia on the first two trips, they bury their assets for safe keeping before going back for more. And then the adventurers disappear on a third trip, perhaps killed by Indians.

But where to bury it in Virginia? Certainly not Lynchburg! That could lead people to us! Old trails and wagon routes from the west—Fincastle and points—would go across the Blue Ridge Mountains and pass through Bedford County. The tale-makers decide on Bedford County.

Byron cautions that the story must be plausible. There is a likelihood of including something that a reader may realize is factually untrue. The story needs to be carefully constructed, without detectable flaws.

Even the details must be credible. The story would have to jibe with logic and history. The adventurers must seem realistic. Ambrose and Henrietta—dear, widely-read Henrietta—agree to be principal authors, putting the ideas onto paper. They weave a tapestry of almost truth. Byron, Eliza, Caleb and David are devil's advocates to test the believability of the story.

They build the story around a "handsomest man" leader character whom they name Thomas J. Beale, a person none of them had known, other than in a legend that floated around town about a former Fincastle man who dueled with the then Botetourt Commonwealth Attorney James Beverly Risque some sixty years or so ago and then left town. To lend relevance to their fiction, they have "Beale" visiting a real Lynchburg lodging house run by a respected gentleman. They attribute much of the narration to lodge owner Robert Morriss, who died more than two decades earlier and therefore cannot contradict their story.

Ambrose, a fan of Edgar Allen Poe's *The Gold Bug*, suggests using encrypted messages to tell part of the story. They decide on three different sets. One special set would be already "solved," establishing that there is a treasure to be found within four miles of Buford's. Another set of ciphers nobly alludes to naming legitimate claimants of the treasure. The third set of ciphers would reveal exactly where it was. Neither of these two unsolved sets of ciphers would be solvable. They would only serve to help create the cover.

Finally, in the fall of 1884, after debating page after page and making refinements, they concur that it is ready for print. Henrietta titles it "The Beale Papers, containing Authentic Statements regarding the Treasure Buried in 1819 and 1821, near Buford's, in Bedford County, Virginia, and Which Has Never Been Found."

Caleb challenges the idea of using Buford's as the burial site. "That's too close to home."

Henrietta replies, "Not really. Yes, the farm is less than four miles from the village store—but the focus is on Buford's Inn, which is miles west from the village. So the farm is outside the four-mile area."

Ambrose expresses his concern, "We don't want anyone to know that we made up this story."

Henrietta asserts, "We could get someone else to deal with the printer—someone who will keep his mouth closed and not expose us."

Agreed, but who?

Henrietta enlists James Beverly Ward, a tall, gaunt and elderly fellow Marshall Lodge Mason of her husband and Byron, to act on her behalf. She explains that she is the author and wants to remain anonymous. Ward, a grandson of James Beverly Risque, is a respected, honorable and naturally taciturn family man. He agrees to deal with the printer and apply for the copyright in his name. He vows never to reveal her name nor embellish or explain the pamphlet's printed story.

The Virginia Book and Job Print Company of Lynchburg, operating again after a fatal fire in 1883, sets the type and runs off a copy for the group to proofread. It becomes a pamphlet with 21 pages. They check it and correct some typographical errors, but do not fret too much if they miss some. It is, after all, just fiction.

Finally, the pamphlets are printed and offered to the public, priced at fifty cents, an amount which could buy a full-course dinner. Its publication attracts some attention in Lynchburg. Some folks believe that a treasure exists, because the "solved" ciphers say so. Others, more skeptical, scoff.

After a few months, the pamphlet falters as a moneymaking publishing venture. One store offers it for half price. Quietly the team retrieves the original papers from the printer and buys up most copies and destroys them. The project is a business failure. But its objective has been accomplished: the tale of a buried treasure near Buford's is etched in the minds and agendas of treasure hunters. And the solution to the ciphers will elude cryptographers forever.

The ciphers make no sense. They are intentionally inscrutable. Surely they will not lead anyone to Meadow Valley Farm. The collaborators worry nevertheless.

Suppose someone accidentally finds the barn cache? If they dig it up, they would find not ingots or nuggets but actual coins with dates in the mid 1800's, well after the story's 1822 scenario. The story of "Beale" could be exposed as a lie. And since the coins were minted and dated before 1865, folks might suspect a link to the Confederate Treasury and ultimately expose the team.

Months pass by and interest in the Beale Papers cools down. No report surfaces about a big treasure find. They are now free. But free to do what?

The collaborators are still tempted to dig up and divide those Confederate assets among themselves.

Byron, ever the conscience, gently but firmly reminds them, "Of course we could strengthen our family businesses and improve the farm. But remember that Trenholm entrusted us to be shepherds for the people's assets. Share them with people who need help. Help our state, our community."

They look at each other. Ambrose agrees, "We must remember where this came from."

Caleb puts it bluntly, "Let's use it all for the loan fund we talked about."

Ambrose points out, "Of course. We four can always borrow from the fund—as long as we pay it back just as anyone else will have to do."

Byron says, "Let's think this through. We need a plan we agree upon."

Ambrose has learned they need to be patient. "Whatever we do, we must not draw attention. If the truth comes out, there could be demands that the wealth was national treasure and the Federal government would seize it. And worse, we would appear to be some sort of swindlers who betrayed a trust. That said, let us proceed. We will have to actually move to Lynchburg about 400 pounds of coins and jewelry. Where and how can we do that without attracting attention? Can we leave the coins as they are—telltale dates and all? Or should we use some sort of makeshift forge in Caleb's barn to melt them down into untraceable ingots? Think about that. What options do we have? When we next get together, bring your ideas on how to make an invisible transfer of these assets."

# CHAPTER 16

## *Transfer*

Caleb comes to Lynchburg for board meetings with Ambrose, Byron, Eliza and Henrietta. Behind closed doors, they explore ideas for secretly bringing the assets from the barn to Lynchburg and then putting it to use.

Ambrose, ever the chairman, leads off, "Remember the big fire here just a few years ago? Best we not risk losing it all. I think it would not be wise to keep it all in one place. We could store half of it at my bank and half in the safe at Byron's office."

Byron agrees, "That makes sense. We can bring it over a bit at a time. Caleb, you could carry maybe three or four pounds or so in your pockets, and so could Ambrose, David and I. In a few months, if we each made two trips, we can bring over maybe twenty-five or thirty pounds."

Henrietta picks up, "Don't leave us out. Eliza and I usually travel with a big bag: we could tote maybe five or six pounds per trip."

Eliza adds, "And we sometimes bring extra clothes and the like in a travel trunk. If the trunk carried an extra ten or twelve pounds, it wouldn't seem unusual."

Ambrose has been adding it up. "All right. Two ladies two trips bring maybe sixty or seventy pounds. We four men, two trips each, maybe twenty-five or thirty pounds. That adds up to about 100 pounds. We would still need to find a way to bring over the other 300."

Caleb proposes, "We could make more trips."

Henrietta says, "Here's another idea. We could mix the coins in with farm products and ship it to Rugerman's warehouse."

"Good idea," responds Byron, "but we would have to package it so that no one guesses what is going on. The packages or crates can't get too heavy. And they should be opened only by one of us."

"How much are we talking about, in a crate?" inquires Ambrose.

Henrietta has been working it out in her head. "Pack a crate with twelve quart-size containers, two layers of six. Label the crate '12 quarts of applesauce, or peaches'—or whatever. Actually, only the top layer will be food quarts—six quarts weighing, maybe...Caleb, what does a quart weigh?"

"A little over two pounds. Six quarts might add up to about fifteen pounds."

Henrietta continues, "The lower layer would be six opaque quarts, each holding ingots, made by Caleb's melting, or gold coins. We would limit each to about the same weight as the produce quart, maybe about two and a half pounds per quart. That would total about fifteen pounds."

Ambrose calculates, "Fifteen pounds of gold would be worth about $3,500."

Caleb nods, "Each crate would have a total of about thirty pounds. That is not suspicious. I could ship them by train to Rugerman's."

Ambrose expands, "Twenty crates would do it. Three hundred pounds of gold, I mean."

Byron likes it. "Treasury assets from the barn could travel to Lynchburg as 'farm produce,' shipped from time to time to my attention, me only, at Rugerman's Wholesalers in Lynchburg. As we go along, I'd bring some over to the bank.

Ambrose could gradually introduce the assets onto the books and into the Community Fund."

Henrietta nods several times, "Ambrose and I will personally adjust the books, with most of the inflow attributed to 'Anonymous' philanthropists." She laughs. "This is like embezzling—only backwards!"

Ambrose interrupts. "That's fine. We also have to do something about the jewelry."

Byron muses. "I'd like Eliza to have a piece of that. Henrietta, too."

Eliza beams at Byron and slowly shakes her head. "No. It's not ours. I wouldn't feel right about it."

Henrietta agrees, "And you might meet someone who once donated it."

Byron nods, "True. But someday I hope I can give Eliza something really special."

"There's plenty of time for that," Eliza remarks, giving her husband one of her sweet smiles.

"Let's talk about how to convert the jewelry into money that can be used. We will have to sell it all," says Ambrose.

"But how? Where?" asks Caleb.

"Not here. Not in Virginia. The jewelry is very elegant, very unique—easily recognized."

Eliza, normally not one to intentially mislead anyone, offers, "Here's one way. When any of you or us are traveling out of state, take a piece along and visit a jeweler or two. Explain that it is a family heirloom, and the family lost their home in the war and needs money. Get a good price."

"Eliza, that could take some time to sell it all," says Caleb.

"Just as well," counsels Ambrose, "that would not attract attention."

Byron suggests, "David can do it as he travels. He travels more than the rest of us. After a while, he'll know values and will get the most for it. Of course, he'll have to make up a good story about each piece he offers for sale. He made up good stories back in Richmond!"

Eliza schedules a visit to the farm in early July to help sister-in-law Hannah preserve some of the early Meadow Valley Farm harvests: beans, berries, and early peaches. With or without gold, this was an annual ritual.

Preserve the food, yes. But this year, it will be a little different. Some would be for family, surely, some would be for market, and some would be for moving gold assets. Hannah still knows nothing about the Treasury reserve. Eliza will arrange chores so Hannah can be diverted while Eliza fills dark jars and packs them in crates.

She knows Byron can manage in Lynchburg without her while she is gone; daughter Martha and son Daniel, who are learning the business at Byron's office, will see that he isn't neglected. Eliza looks forward to days at the farm. For her, farm chores bring back warm memories of her girlhood.

At the Lynchburg station, Byron hugs her goodbye. "You enjoy your time away from this city. But I'll miss you. I'll join you next Friday. Meet me at the train at midday."

She assures him, "I'll miss you, too. I'm off for a few days of fun!"

It doesn't turn out that way.

Eliza and Hannah are cooking and canning. Hannah says, "I'm not complaining, but this is a right tight kitchen, especially when that wood stove is going full draft."

"Caleb told me that he had been thinking about adding a wing. Then you'd get a bigger kitchen. I'll remind him, Hannah!"

"I miss my girls, though I don't know how we'd all fit in here to work! They've gotten to the age where they are really quite good help. You know, Eliza, my sister's new twins are wearing her out. She could use their help a few more days, I'm sure. I would imagine that Beth and Anne would rather be helping with those babies than the hot work of canning. I miss them though."

Eliza assigns herself the job of attaching labels and loading crates. She coaxes Hannah to go to the village for supplies whenever she needs privacy. Then she retrieves coins from the barn which Caleb had excavated and stored for her there. And into the specially labeled containers they go.

On Wednesday night, Hannah and Eliza share a good feeling about a job well done. There are rows of jars for the farm and two stacks of crates. Eliza comments, "Look at all those beautiful, full jars. They'll help you all through the winter. And these eight crates—Byron can take them back to Lynchburg on Monday. We certainly have been productive."

"Eliza, it's been so nice working with you. Mostly we're just glad that you are here."

"I really enjoy visiting you, Caleb, and your wonderful family. Each time I come, we build new good memories. Thanks for letting me be here. It's so refreshing."

"I'm glad."

"Byron is coming on Friday's train. I'd like to celebrate. I think I'll make a cake tomorrow."

"I'd love to do the icing. May I?"


On Thursday morning, Caleb and his boys are up early to check and repair the fences. Caleb sends his sons to the north boundary while he checks the west.

Hannah takes the buggy to the village to get some dye for a cake icing, see if there is any mail, and catch up on community news.

After cleaning up the breakfast dishes and tidying the house, Eliza sets out the mixing bowl, measures out some flour, and then remembers that all the eggs were eaten at breakfast. She wipes her hands on her apron, picks up a small bowl and heads for the chicken coop on the side of the barn.

Almost there she sees the barn door is open. She thinks to herself, "The men wouldn't have done that."

She calls out, "Hello? Anyone in there? Caleb?"

There is a clank, like someone has dropped a heavy tool.

"Hello? Who's there?"

# CHAPTER 17

## *Intruder*

Eliza steps cautiously into the barn.

"Mr. Hallock! What are you doing here! What were you doing with that shovel?"

"I heard about that Beale's Treasure. It's here. You Cornishes stole it. I want some of it!"

"Well it's not. And you get out of here, right now!"

He steps toward her and grabs her. "And I want you!"

"Stop that. Let go. Get away!"

Hallock shoves her down on a hay pile. He falls on top of her and tears at her blouse.

"Help! Caleb! Help!" She flails at him with her hands and fists, dragging fingernails across his face and neck. While he tries to control her hands, she twists and turns her body trying to unseat him. Eliza gets out another scream which draws a harsh slap across the face from Hallock. He finally grabs her wrists and pins her down. She spits in his face and continues to struggle. Momentarily he loosens his grip on one hand. She swings a fist wildly at his face and catches his left eye. She starts another scream which he stops with his hand over her mouth. His grip becomes like a vise on her wrist. With her free hand, she digs her fingernails repeatedly across Hallock face and pulls at his beard.

It seems like an eternity to Eliza before Caleb comes bursting into the barn. He roars, "You bastard! Get off my sister!"

Hallock turns around to get up on one knee and reaches for the shovel to fend off Caleb. Caleb dives at Hallock and grabs him around the neck. The men roll and flail. Hallock is bigger, but Caleb is stronger. Hallock punches Caleb in the sides and back and knees him in the groin. Caleb holds on and squeezes and squeezes. Hallock thrashes…and then goes limp.

"Oh, Caleb," sobs Eliza, "Oh, Caleb!"

Caleb pushes Hallock's body away. He helps Eliza stand up. They cling to each other silently. Eliza is shaking.

Caleb's sons burst through the open door and stop, startled. Edward says, "What's going on? We heard screaming, saw you run to the barn. We got here as quick as we could."

Seeing his usually tidy aunt roughly disheveled, Thomas asks, "Aunt Eliza, are you all right? Why is Mr. Hallock lying there?"

Neither Caleb nor Eliza answers.

Eliza begins to sob all over again, clinging to big brother Caleb. He continues to hold her. Slowing rubbing her back, he tells her, "You're going to be all right. It's going to be all right. It's over."

The boys step closer and stare at Hallock.

Eliza sobs quietly and turns her head and gawks at the man on the floor. "I hate him. He's evil, evil, evil. I hope he goes to Hell."

"Evil, yes. No longer a problem here. He will go to Hell. Eliza, it is all over. Never mind him. Come on, we're going to the house so you can freshen up."

"Boys, Hallock is dead. Don't you do anything. Don't touch him. Wait outside the barn. Don't let anybody in. Don't tell anyone anything. Nothing at all. I'll be back in a few minutes and will explain. Wait for me."

Caleb and Eliza walk slowly to the house and enter through the kitchen door. Hannah is not yet back from the village. Eliza stares blankly at the cake mixings.

"I was making a cake for Byron," she says dully. "I'll finish it, but I need some eggs. Would you tell Thomas to please bring me four or five?"

Caleb again embraces his sister, "Sure, Eliza. Yes. That's a good idea. But first, why don't you freshen up. You'll feel better. Then make the cake. Byron will like that."

"What about that terrible man?"

"He's dead. The boys and I will take care of him. Right now, you rest a bit if you like, then freshen up. The cake can be made when you're ready. And when Hannah gets home, she'll ice it. We'll get your eggs. I'll be back in a few minutes."

At the barn, Caleb tells the boys, "Hallock attacked Aunt Eliza. I fought him." He pauses, takes a deep breath and says, "I killed him."

"He deserves it!"

"This is family business. We must not get the neighbors, or anyone else, involved. Don't even tell your sisters. We've got to avoid any more trouble. Now I need you to help me bury the body. Will you do that?"

"Yes," Edward says.

"Right," says Thomas. "Bury him and forget him. But where?"

"In the barn, below the floor. Let's do it right now, and get it done with."

Caleb picks up a shovel and scrapes an outline of where to dig. The boys are unaware that only a few feet away is a cache of Treasury assets.

The ground is hard, but the boys are strong. They make a good hole in about three minutes. Caleb studies for a moment and says, "Better go down another foot."

When the boys reach the depth, Caleb and Thomas drag Hallock's heavy, limp form and push it into the hole. Thomas and Edward quickly shovel dirt back over the body. Hands shaking, Caleb uses a hoe to smooth the pile. "Bring some dry dirt from over there by the coop. Heap it up a bit. And stomp on it. It's going to settle in a few weeks."

With that done, they spread hay atop it all.

That evening, Caleb and Eliza take a long walk, arm in arm, saying very little.


Caleb meets Byron's arrival on the midday train. The men shake hands.

"Didn't Eliza come? "

"No, she's busy at the house. Come, let's go."

As their buggy clears the depot area, Byron muses, "This is the first time I've gotten off the train here when old Hallock wasn't around! Has he moved away?"

"No. He's dead."

"What? Somebody finally got fed up with his strangeness? Somebody shoot him for being a peeping Tom?"

"I killed him."

"What? You? Killed him?"

"He was attacking Eliza so I killed him."

"Eliza? Not Eliza! How is she? Is she hurt? Hurry! When did this happen? Where? How did you do it?"

"She was only shaken up. She is doing well. You're coming at just the right time. She really misses you. Only my family knows anything about it. Considering it all…she's doing all right. It happened yesterday. He's dead. He's buried. The boys and I buried him."

"How did it happen?"

"She had gone to the barn and found Hallock inside, digging. He said we had the Beale treasure and he wanted it. She told him to get out and then he attacked her and threw her down. She screamed. I was in the field and heard her so I ran down. I saw him on top of her, so I wrestled..." his voice cracked with emotion. "He was stronger than I expected...and I choked him and choked him." Caleb took a deep breath and let it out. "The boys showed up after he was dead. They know what happened, except for his looking for treasure. They still don't know about the reserve. Neither does Hannah." He pauses for a thoughtful moment. "By the looks of Hallock when I arrived, Eliza had put up a real fight."

"Poor Eliza. My sweet Eliza. That bastard. He deserves to be dead. You did the right thing. Thanks."

They ride, neither talking until reaching the farm entrance. Caleb draws the buggy to a halt and looks at Byron. "I'm sorry. I'm sorry for Eliza. I'm sorry I killed Hallock. But, I'm also not sorry."

Byron responds, "You did the right thing. I can't think of what else could have been done. I don't know what I would have done." Both are quiet. Byron continues, "There are times when a man has no choice. You never know. A man has to do what has to be done."

Caleb absorbs that idea. "I guess that's right. Thank you. But I'm sorry I killed him."


At dinner, Caleb says grace, "Lord God, thank you for your love for us all. Thank you for your protection and guidance. Please bless this food to strengthen our bodies and us to your service. Amen."

For dessert, Eliza brings out the cake. "This is to celebrate Byron being here."

"I haven't seen my name on a cake since I was a little boy. My sixth birthday, I think. Thank you, Eliza. Thank you,

Hannah. And thank you, Caleb, for looking out for my dear wife. And thank you, boys, for helping your father do difficult and important jobs."

After dinner, the family vows to keep secret yesterday's attack of Eliza and the death and burial of Hallock. They agree that Eliza's girls, still away helping their aunt, should be spared any knowledge at all of the sordid event.

# CHAPTER 18

# *Fire*

In late July, the Cornish men are busy building a barn and harvesting hay. Months ago, they had cut the first hay and stored it in the hayloft. The next cut is done, but showers came before they could pick it up. The hay just lies there, damp.

Finally, the sky clears and the sun comes out. Caleb thinks to himself, "One more day of sun may do it."

The next morning, the sun climbs through the thinning haze, but by noon the skies are overcast. Caleb trudges into the hayfield, grabs a fistful of hay, sniffs it, and rubs it in his hands.

The boys, Thomas and Edward, are bracing the heavy posts which define the new barn. Caleb interrupts them and calls them over. "The hay is still a little bit damp, but we best get this inside before more rain ruins it completely."

Edward remarks, "The loft is almost full; there's not much open space in the barn. I wish the new one was ready."

"Well, it's not. Pick it up. Pack it in the old barn where you can. Keep the center floor open so there's still room for us to store the carriage and do indoor work."

The boys bring in almost a full wagon load to the old barn They carefully create a compact pile. It fills a quarter of the floor.

They forget that, deep in the pile, uncured hay can generate heat, heat which could ignite the hay in spontaneous combustion. No mind, they move back to the setting up of posts for the new barn.

Caleb begins digging in the barn with the door closed when he hears faint rumbles of a summer thunderstorm coming from the west.

He hears Thomas and Edward pounding nails into the purlins across the posts at the new barn. "Good. A few more weeks and we will finally have that bigger barn."

Caleb is doing his Treasury job: extracting coins from the "bank." He puts them in a small box. Ambrose had figured that after today, there would only be about thirty pounds of coins still in the ground. A cool breeze sneaks through cracks in the walls.

Today, Caleb also selects five or six pieces of jewelry for David to try to sell. He wraps them in a kerchief from his pocket and closes the jewelry bag.

He restores the dirt, stomps it down, and brushes the floor with hay. No one could guess that there had been a hole.

When he gets to the house with his box and bag, the breeze has become a gusty wind and the thunder seems louder and almost continuous. Caleb stows the box and bag in the usual hiding place, above the kitchen beam known only to him, to Eliza, and the other Treasury men.

Thomas and Edward come stomping in. The wind blows harder. Thomas tells his father, "It's good the horses are in the corral. They might get a little crazy if they were in the pasture."

Hannah, who had been working on curtains in the girls' room with Annie and Beth, wanders in, "What's all the commotion?" The girls follow her in.

Caleb reassures his family. "Quite a storm seems to be brewing. But we'll be fine. This old place has been here a hundred years and has weathered lots of storms. I think I'll wait it out with a cup of coffee. Anybody else?" Before anyone can respond, lightning flashes.

After each flash, Hannah counts, "One. Two. Three. Four. Five." Then a boom. "That's one mile." And other flash. "One. Two. Three." She is interrupted by a loud boom. And a flash and a crack. And again. Several flashes. Even a buzz sound. And a boom that shakes the house.

The wind attacks the windows and rattles the tin roof. Caleb spreads his arms and gathers his family to himself.

More crashing thunder and pounding wind. In two minutes it is over. The flashes and thunder are moving east. The wind quiets down.

Hannah says it right: "Thank the Lord that's over!" But it isn't.

By the window, Edward exclaims, "The barn's on fire!"

They all rush to the window. Hannah seems stunned. "Oh, dear! Oh, my goodness!"

Caleb orders, "Boys, take the horses to the far side of the corral! Hannah, help me pull out the buggy. Girls, watch for sparks so the fire doesn't spread to the coop or to the house!"

Hannah opens the barn door; inside some of the hay is on fire. Caleb grabs the reins and harness gear and throws them into the buggy. He pushes and Hannah pulls. Just in time. The flames expand and swell inside the barn and then swirl out the door, chasing the smoke upwards. Sparks lofted by the updraft drift away from the building, toward the wet hayfields.

The hen house, chicken coop and the beginnings of the new barn are safe.

Caleb shakes his head. "It must be God's will." Then, through his teeth, he decides, "It's going to burn and we can't do anything about it."

The entire family watches with awe and fascination, walking here and there for a better view.

Neighbors arrive. Roger Luck speaks first, "We saw the smoke. Are you all all right?"

"Yes. Thanks. And our animals are, too."

Gibbo Overstreet speaks for the group, "What are you going to do? Can we help?"

"Well, thank you. We have got a new barn started, so now we'll just to have to hurry it up."

Frank Hazelgrove says, "I can help you. If I come especially early, I could work a few hours each day before my chores." Three other men nod, "Count on us, too."

"I've got extra hay if you be needing some," says Macon Hatcher.

"That would be good. Thank you all."

The Cornishes feel blessed that neighbors have promised to be there first thing in the morning.

By late evening, the fire is no longer spectacular, just smoldering The burning timbers radiate their red glow over the piles of debris. An acrid smell is everywhere, even in the house.

At last, it is time to go to bed. Caleb says, "We'll make it. We lost the hay and some tools. But when it cools down we can salvage metal things: hinges, hooks, latches for the new barn. We'll miss the old barn, but we can get through."

To himself, he thinks, That was a funeral pyre, that's what that was. Glad I got some coins and some jewelry out. Digging out the rest may be a problem. Anyone would see. Glad I don't have to solve that now.

And to the family, "Tomorrow we work on the new barn."


That night in Lynchburg, there was a loud demanding knock at the back door. Eliza wiped her hands on her apron and went to answer it.

She opened it to find Clinton Hallock. He pushed his way in, grabbing her wrist, saying, "So when's your husband coming home?" Eliza furtively grabs the knife she's just been using, slipping it out from under the pile of apple peelings. She pulls away and plunges the knife into his chest. He just laughs and pulls the knife out. He raises it menacingly. She backs away and screams.

Eliza yelps as she awakens from the nightmare, and Byron firmly takes hold of her arm. She is shaking. Her heart is pounding.

After a moment, she is able to speak, "It was just a dream! Oh, it seemed so real!" As she tells him the dream, her voice transitions from terror to relief.

"I know Hallock is dead. But that was so real. Will he ever really be gone?"

Byron holds her gently and reassures her, "Yes, he is really and truly gone. He will never be back."


In the morning, at the farm, Caleb walks out to look at the ruins. The smell brings back memories of the last hours of Richmond. He writes a brief message and asks Hannah to go to the village and send it as a wire to Ambrose and Byron. It says, "Lightning burned down barn. Nobody hurt. Nothing valuable lost. Neighbors help with new barn."

To himself he says, Life sure is interesting. Somehow, whenever we get a new problem, the Lord shows us the way. We are very blessed.

His faith is soon to be tested again.

# CHAPTER 19

## *Baltimore*

David Rugerman dies in August.

On his third business trip to Baltimore and his second visit to Bowling Jewelers, David enters the handsome, den-like store through an ornate door with beveled glass and gleaming brass hardware. The tinkle of a small bell on the door announces his presence.

Proprietor Marcus Bowling turns and greets him and, after some small talk, places a shallow black velvet tray atop the display case near the front of the store. David pulls a padded satin bag from his valise and spreads an elegant necklace onto the velvet. The low-angle afternoon sun reaches through the window and highlights the gems of the "family heirloom" David is trying to sell for "a client back in Virginia." Mr. Bowling pulls out his loupe and examines the larger stones, holding them up to the light.

"This is a lovely, truly lovely, piece, Mr. Rugerman. If I didn't already have a necklace quite similar, I would be most pleased to buy this from you. However, I don't require both at the same time. No lady likes to believe that someone else has a piece of jewelry that duplicates her own—even if they aren't exactly alike! Tell you what. If you aren't able to find another buyer for it on this trip, bring it back next time. By then, I may have a space in my display case for it. Thank you for bringing it by. That pearl and emerald bracelet you brought in last time sold well."

"Very well, sir. It is always a pleasure to speak with you about beautiful merchandise. I'll look you up next time I'm here in Baltimore. By then this piece will likely be placed elsewhere, but I may have something from another client. Until next time," David closes the valise with the necklace securely inside its satin bag and reaches across the counter to shake hands with Mr. Bowling. "Thank you for your courtesy, sir."

While they are discussing the necklace, several people stop outside the window and peer at the jewelry of precious metals and gems that are on display. One large man, with a brimmed black hat low over his eyes, lingers while the others come and go. He is less interested in the window displays than the activity in the store. He sees only the necklace being discussed. When he sees David place it in his valise, he slips away from the window.

David Rugerman puts his finely woven straw hat back on as he leaves the store. He fails to notice the stranger watching where he goes.

That evening David finishes his dinner and retraces his steps toward his hotel, still clutching his valise. As he walks along Paca Street, he hears a commanding voice, "Halt."

He obediently stops, only to be accosted by the burly man still wearing his black hat low, who jumps out and pulls David into Welcome Alley.

The attacker grabs the valise, but David holds on. With his other hand, David tries to push the man away. The robber punches David in the face and knocks him to the ground. David still clings to the valise. The attacker hits again and with his full weight rams his knee into David's lower chest. Breath gone, David releases his grip.

The assailant searches David's pockets and takes his watch and billfold. He snatches the valise, then steps on David's chest, and runs away down the alley.

David's heart stops beating.

A passerby happens to notice a hat on the brick walk and a pair of feet protruding from the alley. He sees an inert figure lying face up.

"Must be a drunk who passed out. I'll tell the beat cop about it."

When the policeman arrives, he smells no odor of alcohol and sees the man's pockets are inside out. The man is not breathing. He is apparently dead.

The coroner concludes that David died from a crushing chest injury. Police find his calling card in an inner pocket of his jacket and send word back to Lynchburg.

Byron can't believe it, doesn't want to believe it. But it is true. David is dead. Though 45, David was still his little brother. He was such a good man. Wouldn't hurt anybody. Byron moans, "Lord, why did you let this happen?"

The funeral in Lynchburg is a small family affair. Bachelor David has no heirs. Only Byron and his son Daniel remain to carry on the Rugerman name.

Now just five people know about the Confederate reserve Treasury: Ambrose, Byron, Eliza, Caleb, and Henrietta.

# CHAPTER 20

## *Prosperity*

In the fall of 1887 Lynchburg, a city of almost 25,000 people, is bustling on its way to its prewar economic vitality. Local business people admire the leadership and initiatives of both Colonel Bothwell and Captain Rugerman who are part of that progress.

The Rugerman Company is thriving. Suppliers and customers alike trust Byron for his integrity. He pays his suppliers promptly. He is patient with his customers when they are in a pinch. His employees are dedicated to him.

A visitor strolling through the city might not realize that the special Community Fund provided seed money that nurtured fledgling businesses—including Southern Shoes, New Era Pump Manufacturing, Virginia Health Nostrums, and the Rogers Furnishings Emporium. Prudent loans were repaid quickly, freeing the funds to be loaned again to other enterprises.

There were even outright grants which helped start the new Marshall Bradley Hospital and subsidize the Covenant Kitchen meal program.

The Community Fund, managed by the Mountain City Deposit Trust Company, is both generous and demanding. Ambrose Bothwell and his team of advisors rigorously scrutinize those who want a loan or grant—yet will ask "Are you sure that's enough?" Ambrose insists upon specific goals, verified references and repayment schedules. He monitors their progress. If they start to fall short he calls them in and asks, "What's the problem?" He helps them work out their troubles, believing it is better to help them than to shut them down.

Shortly after lunch one October day, into Ambrose's office steps Judge William Robinson, brilliant law graduate of Washington and Lee—tall, lean, with wire spectacles framing twinkling eyes—known and esteemed as tough but fair.

"Good morning, Ambrose. Do you have a moment?"

"Of course, Judge. What can I do for you?"

"Are you aware that Governor Fitzhugh Lee is coming to town to visit our Fair?"

"Yes, I heard something like that. In a fortnight, I believe. The city's looking forward to that. Governor Lee is a favorite here."

"I returned yesterday from a Judicial Conference at the Capitol. The Governor told me he wants to meet you."

"Me? Why?"

"Well, when the conference ended, Governor Lee asked me about you. He said he'd heard about the good work of the Fund. He wants to talk with you when he's here."

"I'm honored. I'll be available any time that suits him."

The judge leans closer, and says, confidentially, "He wants to know your secret. I do, too."

"Secret?"

"Yes, how the Fund has grown as it has. Is that all from plowed back interest?"

"Well, no, to tell the truth."

"Then, how?"

"The Fund has grown because of an infusion of capital."

"From where?"

"Well, Judge, there have been anonymous sources."

The judge persists. "Lynchburg folks?"

126

"No, to be honest, I'll just say good friends—who want no attention."

The judge steps back, "All right. You cover them well."

Smiling, Ambrose ends it, "This is a Trust company!"

Ambrose and Judge Robinson continue to chat amicably, but Ambrose is barely listening. He is thinking about meeting the Governor.


At the Fair, Ambrose introduces himself to Fitzhugh Lee. "Judge Robinson said you wanted to see me."

"Yes. Ambrose—may I call you Ambrose?"

"Of course, Governor."

"I've been hearing good things about your bank and The Community Fund. This state needs men like you who care about people and who know how to manage money and get real results. People who know what they are doing."

"Those are kind words, Governor."

"What I want you to do is this: come see me in Richmond so we can have a real good talk."

"About what, sir?"

"I want your ideas about how you might run the State Treasury office."

For a moment—a long moment—Ambrose pauses for the right response. Then, "Yes, we could talk. When would it be convenient for you, sir?"

"I've got some more appointments around the State, but I promised Mrs. Lee that I will celebrate Thanksgiving in Richmond. How about the week after that?"

"Yes, sir."

"Good. Set it up with my aide, Jonathan Wilkes, over there, and set a date."

"Yes, sir."

The Governor begins a conversation with another constituent.

Ambrose feels honored.

He joins up with Byron. "The Governor wants to talk to me about the State Treasury. Maybe run it."

"Mmmm. He's a wise man. You probably could do a better job than that fellow who is in there now. With your gray hair, you even look like a cabinet member. Will you go see him?"

"Yes, I will. About December first. And I'll try to understand all I can before I get there."

"I guess you better start studying!" Byron pauses and says, "You know, Ambrose, I had a significant inquiry as well."

"What?"

"Mayor Manson approached me and said that Congressman Samuel Hopkins—he's a former Confederate Marylander, you know, not a real Lynchburg man—is retiring at the end of his term next year. He has already announced that he will not stand for reelection next year. Plans to focus solely on his mercantile business."

"And?"

"The Mayor asked me if I would consider running."

"What did you say?"

"I said I'd have to talk with Eliza about it. And you."

"Why me?"

"Well, you may be my cousin, but you've been more like a big brother for maybe fifty years...." Ambrose interrupts, "Forty-nine, actually." Byron continues, "I'm not sure that I could get along without us talking together the way we do."

"You don't need me. You have more gray hair than I do—you would be treated with respect!"

"You underestimate how much your counsel has helped me."

128

"Likewise. I must admit that if I go to Richmond, I'll miss your advice. They say that in politics the advice you get is almost never objective, never unbiased. Everybody is trying to promote his own interests. Everyone is telling stories to suit some obscure purpose. It's endemic."

"But isn't much of life like that? Haven't we done some of that, too? You could handle it. You're good at sorting out the truth."

"And so are you, Byron. But, you know, when I was younger, I was pretty certain I knew the answers, that I was an accurate judge of character. But after my experience with that Alderson fellow—who absconded with the money—I'm not so sure. Now I'm a bit more cynical—and doubt my own ability."

"I guess that comes with age, Ambrose. I've been feeling that, too. I realize that things rarely are as they seem—and I have to be more careful before deciding something. Maybe the Lord intends it to be so. Too much confidence needs to be tempered with humility." Byron pauses, "As for the future? I don't know. I guess we each have a lot to think about."

"I'll have to evaluate who would lead the bank and fund work if I left to spend a fair amount of time in Richmond."

"And I'd have to make sure my business could continue while Congress would be in session in Washington. Eliza has gotten used to city life here. Washington would just be bigger. I asked her if big city life would worry her; there are so many stories of crime there. But she isn't fazed. In fact, she told me, 'Life on a farm can be dangerous, too!' And she knows better than most! She and I may scout the capital—to see what life is like there. We could visit that Washington Monument now that it's finally finished."

"Fortunately, we both have smart wives and we both have good folks working for us. We've been blessed to have some of our children helping us. It's about time they took more of the responsibility for the total operations."

"And maybe do better than us!"

"Let's hold up any big decisions until after Thanksgiving."

"Agreed."

# CHAPTER 21

# *Thanksgiving*

Caleb Cornish, now 48, and Hannah, 40, host this gathering of families for Thanksgiving dinner at the Valley Meadow Farm. The house easily accommodates the fourteen who gather in the great room which is almost as big as the entire old log house that had served earlier generations. Helping to prepare the meal are daughters Beth, 17, and Annie, 15. Sons Thomas, 20, and Edward, 18, are tending the sheep and horses.

Eliza and husband Byron Rugerman arrived by train from Lynchburg the night before with their spinster daughter, Martha, 27, a teacher, and son Daniel, 25, a friendly young man who works for his father. The Rugermans are a handsome, prosperous family.

The well-dressed Bothwells, Ambrose, now 51, and Henrietta and their beautiful twins, Sarah and Mary, 21, arrive that morning and are greeted at the depot by Thomas driving the Cornish's modern covered carriage. On the way to the farm, they pass and ignore the abandoned Hallock place.

The young people stroll outside or sit on the swings under the giant chestnut trees and swap stories about their plans and social engagements. The women share family news as they finish preparing the food and setting the table. The men sit on the porch, admiring the view of the valley and the mountains while talking business.

Caleb has increased his herd of sheep to almost 150 and his boys have recently finished the hayloft doors on the new barn, close to the charred remnants of the old one. Ambrose says he has been busy training capable new people to handle his bank's expansion. Byron reports that son Daniel is of real help now, and his new sales manager is bringing in new clients. Insurance claims are down. Business couldn't be better.

Hannah pokes her head out the front door. "Excuse me, gentlemen. I'm sorry to intrude upon such lofty conversation, but Caleb, could you please go get some wood for the cook stove. We've been cooking up such a storm that I ran out before I expected. You're a dear. Thank you. Dinner will be ready soon, I hope!"

Caleb rises with a little smile on his face, "Small price to pay for the meal we're about eat, I venture." And off he goes to the wood pile.

Ambrose and Byron take this opportunity to stroll away from the house and look down towards the new barn. Ambrose inquires, "Byron, are you going to run for Congress?"

Byron's answer is brief, "Maybe. Eliza and I have been talking about it. We need more time to think it through. What about you? Do you want to be Virginia's Secretary of the Treasury?"

"I might. I'll go see Fitzhugh Lee. But Henrietta and I must understand all the implications. It may be clearer by Christmas."

Approaching dark frontal clouds, bringing a sudden chill to the unseasonably warm November day, prompt them to go inside to join the others.

Soon everyone gathers around the dining room table and sits down. They bow their heads. Host Caleb notes that Thanksgiving first became a national holiday under Yankee Abraham Lincoln. He then acknowledges to God how blessed they are with good health, family, prosperity, and for this "we humbly thank you, Lord."

Then, as all say "Amen," Ambrose quietly murmurs, "And you too, George."

Young Annie looks up in puzzlement, "Who?"

Caleb, Byron and Ambrose exchange quick smiles, and Ambrose replies, "Just an old friend. A good friend."


Beth, with a voice like Hannah's, speaks up, "Father, you didn't notice my new earrings."

"New earrings?"

"Yes, do you like them?"

"I do. They're nice. Where'd you get them?"

"She found them," says Hannah.

"Found them? Where?"

"Beth, tell your father where you found them."

"I found them outside."

"Found them outside?"

"I was out in the corral, talking to the horses, just looking around. I noticed the chickens scratching around, near the ashes. You know, of the old barn."

"So? What about the earrings?"

"Well, one chicken came away from the ashes with the earrings."

"A chicken with earrings! Really—where did you get them?"

"Honestly, Father, this chicken had something shiny dangling from its beak, like it was trying to eat it. I caught up with her and took two earrings from her. They were hooked together and mostly covered with ash. I wiped them off and they were beautiful! Here, look at this one."

"Yes, that is pretty. But strange that a chicken was walking around with earrings! Hannah, has anyone around said they lost earrings?"

"If so, I haven't heard."

Henrietta offers, "Perhaps somebody lost them long ago. Or maybe they were buried back during the war. A lot of people buried valuables so the Yankees wouldn't steal them."

Eliza adds, "Yes, Henrietta. I think Mrs. Rostenberry buried her silverware when Hunter's army was coming. Those Yankees didn't find it!"

"Maybe someone buried valuables right here. How about grandfather and grandmother? Did they do that?" asks Annie.

Eliza cools the idea down, "They didn't have any fancy jewelry to bury."

Caleb interjects, "Girls, girls. That's a romantic idea. Like fiction. Everybody likes a story about buried treasure. What do you think, Ambrose?"

"Caleb, you're right. Sounds like a fantasy. Byron?"

"True treasure is in the heart. Right, Caleb?"

"Right. I would discourage anyone from spending time looking for any buried treasure around here."


The serving dishes have just made a second round of the table when there is a sudden clap of thunder—rare for this late in November—followed by the sound of a horse coming to the house. Eliza rises to refill the turkey platter.

"Someone's here," says Thomas.

"Who is it?" Caleb asks. "Are we expecting someone?"

"I don't know."

"Go to the door, son, and see what they want."

Eliza slips to the front window, peeks out the curtain and gasps. There stands a tall, husky man. Under his dirty hat, she sees a splotchy beard, messy hair, and weathered skin. He senses that he is being observed and looks in her direction with a menacing eye. She turns away and quietly exclaims, "Oh, dear Lord, it's Clinton Hallock himself!"

Thomas goes to the door and returns to announce, "It's a man. Says his name is Hallock."

Eliza gasps again.

"Hallock?" says Ambrose.

The eyes of Caleb, Byron and Ambrose connect. Facial expressions reveal nothing.

"Yes," Thomas says. "He wants to talk to the man of the house. I told him to wait right there on the porch."

"Good. Thank you, son. I'll talk with him."

Caleb rises from his seat and very deliberately slides the chair under the table while he gathers his thoughts. Then he turns and walks briskly to the door.

Gruffly, the stranger inquires, "Are you Mister Cornish?"

"Yes, I'm Caleb Cornish. What can I do for you?"

"I'm William, Clinton Hallock's brother."

"Why are you here?"

"I haven't heard from him for more than a year, so I came to see him. I found where his place was. But it looks like he's been away for a while."

"Yes, he hasn't been seen around for some time. Where are you from?"

"I live outside of Staunton. Clinton never was very good at paying heed to the family. I'm the only one left now."

"And?"

"The folks passed away long ago. Our sister died of small-pox. No kids. I don't know where her husband is. Clinton's wife disappeared years ago. And I ain't never been married. I'm older than him. He's all I got."

"I see," drawls Caleb.

"So I got to wondering about him. Have you seen him?"

"Not lately. Actually, it's been a long time since I last saw him."

"How was he?"

"He didn't look well."

"Where is he now?"

Caleb pauses and scratches his head, "I heard somebody say that they thought he was after that Beale's Treasure. Have you heard of it?"

"Yeah, it's about gold and silver from out West."

"Maybe he went looking for the treasure."

"You haven't seen him lately?"

"No, it's been quite a while, but I do remember him."

"Well, I got no reason to go back to Staunton. I reckon I might just as well stay in his house. Until he comes back. Or until I find out where he went—or what happened to him."

"That's up to you."

"And in the meantime, I'd like to get to know you all real well."

"That's your choice. Take care, Mr. Hallock."

Caleb closes the door as he says, "Happy Thanksgiving."

THE END

# ACKNOWLEDGEMENTS

This novel derives from ideas introduced in my earlier books about the Beale Treasure. It draws from the public record, published works, and from personal conversations.

Organizations whose reservoirs of facts were useful include: Bedford City/County Museum, Bedford Public Library, Jones Memorial Library, Legacy Museum of African American History, Lynchburg Cemetery, Lynchburg Museum, O. Winston Link Museum, Sandusky Foundation, U.S. Navy, and the Virginia Military Institute.

I salute these writers whose works were published decades ago: E.P. Alexander, Christian Asbury, C.C. Buel, C.M. Blackford, W. Asbury Christian, Winston Churchill, Robert M. Coates, Hamilton Cochran, G. Foster, Don P. Halsey, John Horner, R.V. Johnson, R.K. Ketchum, Edward Pollock, F.H.S. Smith, and P.B. Winfree, Jr.

Thanks, too, to authors whose works have been published more recently, including: Chris Bishop, Louise Blunt, W. Harrison Daniel, Ted Delaney, Ian Drury, William D. Edson, Paul Escot, Tom Gibbons, June Goode, Richard Holmes, Peter Houck, Angus J. Johnston, Francis Lord, Judith B.McGuire, Lula J. Parker, Dorothy & Clifton Potter, Phillip Rhodes, Philip Scruggs, Walbrook D. Swank, Jack Trammel, and R.S. Yeoman.

Individuals who shared their time and special knowledge included: Albert Atwell, Casey Brewer, Brian Buchanan, Connie Cordogan, Brian Crosier, Jim Henry, Mark Huffines, Allen Joslyn, Ivan Kirby, Tom Ledford, Bill Middleton, Ken Miller, Mike Nichols, David Sines, Skip Tharp, and Gary Walker. To those whom I overlooked, please forgive me.

My wife, Cyndi, provided ideas, helped hone the story, and typed the manuscript again, and again, and again. Without her, there would be no book. Sister-in-law Amy G. Moore added artistic creations and formatted the text for printing. Linda Kochendarfer gave literary guidance.

Special thanks to Judge William W. Sweeney for his astute critiques of drafts of this book and for his inspiring encouragement.

Any errors in this book are solely my responsibillity.

Peter Viemeister
Bedford, Virginia
2004

# History Books by Peter Viemeister

Read excerpts of any of these fine books at **www.peterv.com**

## *Historical Diary of Bedford, Virginia, U.S.A. — From Ancient Times to the U.S. Bicentennial*

Chronicle of life in the region in peace and war. People and events. Indians. Revolution. List of militia men. Jefferson's Poplar Forest. Civil War. Local Money. Old-time ads. The Depression. D-Day. War Times. The 50's and 60's. Smith Mountain dam. 2500 item index. 256 pictures. 132 big pages. 3rd printing. Cloth Hardcover. ISBN 0-9608508-209

## *History of Aviation — They Were There*

All phases of aviation, from the first balloons to outer space. Personal reports by famous and not famous. Many of the folks were from Virginia. Wide coverage of World War II and Vietnam. With rare photos. Detailed 12-page index. A great gift for any aviation fan. 348 pages. 298 photos. Cloth Hardcover. ISBN 0-9608598-6-1

## *The Beale Treasure — NEW History of a Mystery*

Facts about the story of the gold and silver purportedly buried in Bedford in 1819 and 1821. Here are 54 photos, diagrams and maps, and the complete original pamphlet with the cipher which describe the exact location. Explores possible links to Thomas Jefferson, Jean Lafitte, and the Civil War Confederate treasury. Includes map of known dig sites. This is the authoritative book on the subject. 190 useful references. Big index. 4th printing. Cloth Hardcover. ISBN 1-882912-04-0

*Peaks of Otter — Life and Times*

A history of Virginia and America, with the Blue Ridge Mountains as the stage. Wildlife, Indians, Frontier Days, Civil War, the full story of Union General Hunter's raid, Ghosts and Murders, Herd of Elks, the missing Town, C.C.C. boys, building the Blue Ridge Parkway, and Plane Crashes. 200 illustrations. 278 pages. Full index. 4th printing. Flex Cover. ISBN 1-883912-13-X

*Start All Over — An American's Experience*

From living with Indians to dealing with the rich and powerful, Viemeister reveals the inside story of big corporations, foundations, and local politics. Exciting people and places in the historical, cultural, and emotional settings of the 30's and 40's. World War II home front and rationing. The 50's, the turbulent Vietnam War years and the exicitng 80's and 90's. Count Basie, the Tucker car. Nuclear waste dump. Full index. 241 illustrations. 451 pages. Cloth Hardcover. ISBN 1-883912-01-6

*From Slaves to Satellites — 250 Years on a Virginia Farm*

True story of real people and what happened here—and why—of a typical southern farm; hardy folk coping with the unpredictable. Slavery was commonplace and more prevalent than generally believed: read how even a neighborhood church owned slaves. When slavery ended, the invisible hand of economics drove changes in land use, change in the relationship of landowner to the tenant farmer and sharecropper, and change in the role of the neighborhood church. 60 illustrations. Extensive bibliography. Flex Cover. ISBN 1-883912-06-7

# ABOUT THE AUTHOR

## *Peter Viemeister*

During his almost three decades with Grumman, the firm which produced the craft that landed men on the moon, he served as a mechanic, an engineer, President of Grumman Data Systems, and Vice President – Development of the Grumman Corporation.

He grew up during the Depression and World War II and attended country and suburban public schools, graduated from Rensselaer Polytechnic Institute, and was a Sloan Fellow at M.I.T.

He traveled to Europe, Russia, Mexico, New Zealand, Czechoslovakia, Korea, Cuba, Australia, and the Caribbean. Along the way, he has known special people—some rich, some powerful, and some just wonderful—who gave new insights about life.

He taught Organizational Behavior at two colleges and holds a patent for a Simulator of Human Behavior. His eight books combine clear writing, original research, unusual photos, and rare drawings.

Love of country life led him to Bedford, where he has served as Chairman of the City/County Museum, the Community Health Foundation, and the National D-Day Memorial Foundation. He is a trustee of Lynchburg College and a Regent of Liberty University.